W9-BAD-705

THE TIGER'S APPRENTICE

BOOK TWO
TIGER'S BLOOD

ALSO BY LAURENCE YEP

THE TIGER'S APPRENTICE TRILOGY
The Tiger's Apprentice, Book One
Tiger Magic, Book Three (2006)

GOLDEN MOUNTAIN CHRONICLES

The extraordinary intergenerational story of the Young family
from Three Willows Village, Kwangtung Province, China, and
their lives in the Land of the Golden Mountain—America.

The Serpent's Children (1849)

Mountain Light (1855)

Dragon's Gate (1867)
A Newbery Honor Book

The Traitor (1885)

Dragonwings (1903)
A Newbery Honor Book

The Red Warrior (1939)
Coming Soon

Child of the Owl (1965)

Sea Glass (1970)

Thief of Hearts (1995)

EDITED BY LAURENCE YEP

American Dragons
Twenty-Five Asian American Voices

THE TIGER'S APPRENTICE

BOOK TWO

TIGER'S BLOOD

LAURENCE YEP

HarperCollinsPublishers

Tiger's Blood

Copyright © 2005 by Laurence Yep

All rights reserved. No part of this book may be used or reproduced in
any manner whatsoever without written permission except in the case of
brief quotations embodied in critical articles and reviews. Printed in the
United States of America. For information address HarperCollins
Children's Books, a division of HarperCollins Publishers,
1350 Avenue of the Americas, New York, NY 10019.
www.harperchildrens.com

Library of Congress Cataloging-in-Publication Data
Yep, Laurence.
    Tiger's blood / Laurence Yep.— 1st ed.
        p.   cm. — (The tiger's apprentice ; bk. 2)
    Summary: A Chinese American boy and his friends—a monkey, a dragon,
a rat, and a tiger—must ensure that a magical phoenix egg does not fall into
evil hands in the underwater dragon kingdom.
    ISBN 0-06-001016-9 — ISBN 0-06-001017-7 (lib. bdg.)
    [1. Magic—Fiction. 2. Dragons—Fiction. 3. Chinese-Americans—Fiction.
4. San Francisco (Calif.)—Fiction.] I. Title. II. Series.
PZ7.Y44Tk 2005   2004002704
[Fic]—dc22   CIP
                                                                             AC

Typography by Karin Paprocki
1 2 3 4 5 6 7 8 9 10
❖
First Edition

To my editor, Toni Markiet,
for putting up with me for this many years

PREFACE

C hinese mythology is more than four thousand years old, with its roots stretching even further into the past. The myths and legends of the latest era reflect the orderly human world of imperial China in which gods, spirits, heroes, and even demons belong to a bureaucratic and hierarchic world.

However, the deeper one goes into Chinese mythology, the wilder and stranger the myths become. In the earliest periods, bureaucratic priests, contemplative hermits, and exemplary scholars give way to strange creatures such as the yen huo, the chu chien, the jen-mien hsiao, and the p'ao hsiao, which are all drawn from that ancient Chinese compendium of wonders, *Shan Hai Ching* (ca. third century B.C.). Other creatures are drawn from other ancient classics, the *Lieh Tzu* and the *Shu Ching*.

Monkey, of course, comes from the many tales finally

collected in *The Journey to the West*, but his anarchic spirit belongs to much more primitive times.

Dragons, I believe, belong to the earliest times when the first humans were trying to understand the forces of Nature, which could sometimes be kind and sometimes violently cruel. In time, dragons came to symbolize fertility by bringing rain, and while generally benevolent, the legends also portray them as proud of their privileges, protective of their territory and possessions, and, if truth be told, rather difficult to live with as neighbors.

CHAPTER ONE

※

I f Mistral the dragon and Monkey could have had their way, they would have left San Francisco the next instant for the dragon kingdom, but Mr. Hu would not be hurried with his packing.

So, while an impatient Mistral kept watch in the front of the store, the elderly tiger had the rest of them—Tom, Monkey, and the flying rat, Sidney—hopping about the apartment at the rear of his antique store as they gathered what Mr. Hu considered necessities.

Tom was surprised when he found they were taking few clothes but a good many books and magical apparatus. "Why are we taking so much gear?"

"Because you are to continue your studies in the Lore while you are in the dragon kingdom," Mr. Hu replied.

"But it's summer," the boy protested. "I'm supposed to be on vacation." The promised drudgery was already making Tom rethink staying on as Mr. Hu's apprentice.

The tiger's whiskers twitched. "I can't believe Mistress Lee didn't make you study every spare moment." Mistress Lee was Tom's grandmother and the Guardian before Mr. Hu. "When I was her apprentice, I had lessons year-round."

"Well," the boy admitted, "it's not like she didn't try."

Monkey looked around the stack of books he was carrying. "Tom was also her grandson. I bet he managed to charm his way out of them. Unlike a certain tiger I know who doesn't have enough charm to fill a tea bag."

Mr. Hu gave a harrumph. "Well, there will be no slacking off as *my* apprentice, I can tell you that!"

Monkey shuffled over to a suitcase and began to pile the books inside. "He's a human cub, Hu. You can't expect blind obedience."

The tiger's nostrils and mouth wriggled in interesting ways as he fought to control his temper. "Yes, yes, I suppose so," he finally conceded. "Just keep this in mind, Master Thomas: Evil takes no holidays. You will need every bit of magic if you're to protect yourself the next time we meet Vatten and the Clan of the Nine." The Clan of the Nine were Vatten's monstrous followers.

Vatten had been seeking the egg of the fabulous phoenix for thousands of years, for the phoenix would allow him to change people's wills. His spies, led by his henchmen Loo and a girl named Räv, had even managed to steal it for a while; Mr. Hu, the latest Guardian of the egg, had managed to take it back but only at great cost.

As he remembered some of the monsters they had already faced, Tom realized the one thing worse than the boredom of an apprenticeship—the terror-filled periods when something finally did occur.

"He won't have a chance to learn more magic if we don't leave soon," Mistral called impatiently from the store. "The Clan of the Nine could be here any moment."

"What would happen if Vatten got hold of the egg?" Tom asked. "I mean, I know he'll hatch the egg and use it to control people. So would he make himself the king of the world?"

Around Mr. Hu's neck hung the pouch with the phoenix egg, and he touched it now. "If he were to rule, people would welcome death. He hates humans even more than his master, Kung Kung, who first tried to take the phoenix. Kung Kung found humans distressingly 'disorderly,' so he would have changed them into mindless creatures."

"Like zombies?" Tom gulped.

"I was going to say like automata," Mr. Hu said after thinking for a moment, "but yes, that might be another way to put it. However, Vatten has seen humans overrun the earth and almost ruin it."

"So he'd destroy all humans?" Tom asked.

"His tastes are far crueler," Mr. Hu said. "No, he would make humanity suffer a living nightmare."

"Are you just going to talk or are you going to pack?" Mistral shouted.

They set to work with an even greater sense of urgency after Mr. Hu's description of a world ruled by Vatten, until Monkey finally brought the packing to a halt. "Any more, Hu, and we'll need a truck."

The Guardian looked around the shelves regretfully, as if there were even more books and devices he would have liked to take. He grumbled. "Oh, very well, but I hope Master Thomas does not pay the price for the gaps in his education."

His fur vibrating so that he looked like a fuzzy balloon, Sidney struggled to bring down a huge volume that proved too heavy for him, and he plopped down on the floor with the book on top of him. As a cloud of dust rose, the rat wheezed from beneath the tome. "Geez. Running from Vatten is almost as bad as fighting him."

The tiger's eyelids shot up and his great amber eyes blazed with a little of their old fire. "I have never run from combat in my life. This is a . . ."

Monkey had pulled off his cap and was fanning himself. "A holiday?"

"A strategic retreat," Mr. Hu corrected him with a stern frown.

After the Guardian had called a taxi, Mistral changed from a dragon into a young woman in a suit of shimmering black silk, while Monkey became a small man in a dapper white suit with a fake leopard-skin collar and cap. Mr. Hu transformed into an elderly man in a three-piece suit with a red silk tie and handkerchief to match.

Then Tom helped the tiger go about the building setting up protective wards to keep out their enemies. When they returned to the store, they found the others waiting impatiently, scanning the shadows of the Chinatown alley outside the store for monsters. It was a small sense of relief when the cab pulled up in front.

As Monkey and Sidney began loading suitcases into the trunk, Mistral lifted her head in alarm. "It's Räv!" she whispered anxiously.

Monkey and Sidney stopped loading the suitcases into the taxicab to look in the direction the dragon was pointing.

Mr. Hu was leaning upon his apprentice, Tom. Too weary to turn his head, he twitched his ears like radar dishes; but after listening intently for a moment, he said, "That's impossible. She's trapped in here with the *hsieh*." The hsieh were a pack of monstrous hounds that had ambushed them on Vatten's orders.

"That silver hair was unmistakable," Mistral insisted.

Though the Guardian had every confidence in his spells, Räv was such a dangerous spy that he hastily dug out of his suit pocket a green rock in which she and the hsieh were trapped. As he examined it between his fingers, he frowned. "Odd, there's a small hole here." He surveyed

5

the alley outside his store. "I wonder . . ."

Tom saw that the smooth surface of the rock was marred by a tiny nick, as if someone had chipped off a piece the size of a pinhead.

Monkey gave up surveying the rooftops for their enemy. "She couldn't have escaped your magic," he reassured the tiger wizard. "I saw her drawn into it with all that pack of hounds."

"Quite so. There couldn't have been a flaw in my entrapment spell. I'm sure they're all having sweet dreams right now." The tiger restored the rock to his pocket. "Even so, we'd better leave as soon as we can."

"I tell you I saw her," Mistral insisted stiffly, as she kept watch for trouble. "We should be expecting an attack any moment."

With a new sense of urgency, Monkey heaved the last suitcase into the trunk with a thump. "This is the last."

As he closed the lid with difficulty, the cabby asked, "Whatcha got in there? The kitchen sink?" His taxi sagged noticeably in the rear.

"Everything but that," Monkey said as he opened the taxi doors.

And, Tom thought, they would have taken that too if Mr. Hu could have worked it into a lesson.

The cabby climbed into the driver's seat, not suspecting that Tom was his only human passenger. The only one who brought a stare from the cabby was Sidney, who proudly insisted on keeping his own shape; but when the enterprising rat tried to sell the cabby some giant dice to hang from the rearview mirror, the driver seemed to decide that Sidney must be human—no matter how hairy. After all, whoever heard of a rat that came up to a man's knee and wore a cap with flaps? The driver muttered something about "darn pushy hippies" and left it at that.

Tom helped Mr. Hu climb into the back, while Monkey and Sidney squeezed into the front seat. With one last scan of the rooftops, Mistral eased into the rear.

"Where to?" the cabby asked them.

To Tom's surprise, Mistral announced, "The Museum of Kelp."

As they rolled out of the alley, the dragon looked left and right, scanning for the attack she was sure was going to come.

Though he had known her for only a few days, the boy had come to like the moody dragon. As they drove through Chinatown, Tom wanted to ask his friend why they were going to a museum instead of to the dragon kingdom, but she was busy keeping watch for Räv and a new horde of attackers.

Even had she not been so preoccupied, he might have hesitated because of her expression. She looked as if she were heading for her own funeral. For even if they reached the dragon kingdom, she was still risking her life. He felt helpless, unsure of what to say to someone who was voluntarily traveling to her possible execution. For insulting the Dragon King, Mistral had been exiled to the land, never to return to the sea on penalty of death, but the homesick dragon was determined to accompany them.

"Are you sure you want to go with us?" he whispered.

"That's my choice, not yours." There was deep sorrow and even deeper pride in her voice as she surveyed the roofs.

"But why?" The words caught in Tom's throat.

Even in her human disguise, there was a power in Mistral's body and voice. "It's one thing if your master questions my decision, but quite another from a young whelp."

Mr. Hu interceded on behalf of his apprentice. "He's young. He doesn't understand." The tiger cast a discreet spell on the cabby so he would not hear them.

Her spine and shoulders still tense with anger, she gazed over Tom's head at the tiger but her words were meant for the boy. "And may he never understand what it is like to spend as many years as I have from his home and his own kind. Besides, I'm not the only one facing punishment." She shot a look at Monkey.

Ages ago, the ape had stolen into the palace of the Dragon King and taken a magic staff. With his usual bravado, Monkey tipped his cap. "Well, I haven't been tried yet, so maybe they'll just thank me for removing some of their trash."

"Trash?" spluttered Mistral. "How dare you label a treasure of the dragon kingdom that!"

"As my companion," Mr. Hu said, "I think the dragons will tolerate him for a short while. But my protection may not extend as far as you, my exiled friend."

"I'm prepared for that." She shrugged. "Now let me go back to watching for our enemies."

Still, Tom was not willing to let the dragon swim to her death, and he appealed to Mr. Hu in a low voice. "Can't you convince her not to go?"

The tiger gazed sadly at the disguised dragon. "She's tired of wandering, and who can blame her?"

Most of Tom's life, his neighbors and schoolmates had shunned him because they thought he was as eccentric as his grandmother, with whom he'd lived. Even at his loneliest, though, he'd had his loving grandmother, and when she died, Mr. Hu made it clear that his Chinatown store was the boy's home as long as he wanted.

"But she's not alone," Tom protested to Mr. Hu. "She's got us."

"It's her choice," Mr. Hu said quietly. "We must respect that."

Tom thought to himself that he would never let a friend go to her death.

"Just like it was my grandmother's?" Tom asked in a husky voice. His grandmother had sacrificed her own life so that Tom and Mr. Hu could escape with her precious treasure, the phoenix egg, which Mr. Hu now wore in a pouch around his neck.

"Yes," Mr. Hu said grimly. "People must sometimes make hard choices, and Guardians most of all." He had said much the same thing when he had imprisoned Räv. But had he succeeded? The girl had proven very clever.

Tom scanned San Francisco for some sign of the silver-haired spy who was so dangerous and yet so contradictory. She had stolen the phoenix egg from him, but she had also prevented him from being killed. Surely that meant she wasn't as evil as her master, Vatten. Sternly he reminded himself that she had reverted to her old habits when she had later drawn them into a deadly ambush by the hsieh. If she had managed to escape, she was probably leading more of the Clan of the Nine to attack them.

All he saw, though, were ordinary scenes on familiar streets—people shopping, businessmen and -women hurrying to some appointment, a meter maid writing a ticket—but that brought little comfort. He now knew what these innocent folk did not: that a monster might be lurking in the darkness of the nearest doorway.

"I guess the odds are long against us," Tom said.

Mr. Hu clasped his paws over his lap. "No, the odds were far greater against the first Guardian, Surefoot. It took the efforts of every dragon and hero to stop Kung Kung—first from seizing the phoenix for his own twisted ends, and then, when he was thwarted in his first goal, to keep him from destroying the world itself. But the war left the world so wasted that the survivors were in dismay and the phoenix himself returned to an egg.

"As Calambac, the first and mightiest of dragons, looked upon the broken earth and counted the cost of all the dead, including his own children, he said, 'What victory is this? And more wars will come because of the phoenix. Who will take up this great burden?'

"'Let me take it,' piped a tiny voice.

"And the dragon swung his head this way and that, gazing all about, but all the weary warriors around him shook their heads, for they had said nothing. 'I hear you, but I do not see you. Are you invisible?'

"'No, Your Highness,' said the voice. 'Look down by your paw, but be careful not to move it.'

"And the dragon looked down and saw the smallest of warriors, Surefoot, with even more wounds on her small body than Calambac.

"'Let me take it,' said the mouse, 'and I will keep this most precious of objects safe.'

"And wizard and hero and all the others laughed, save Calambac, for he had been among the first creatures to wake up and so he had some of the power of foreseeing and said, 'It is fitting that the greatest power should belong to the smallest.' And he won the others over, for there were none purer and more selfless of heart than Surefoot.

"But Calambac, like the others, had assumed Surefoot

would reside with one of them for protection, but she insisted on leaving their protection. 'For,' as she said, 'it's a fine line between protection and imprisonment. And who's to say who will be corrupted by this?'

"It wasn't long before Vatten had rallied Kung Kung's surviving followers and formed the Clan of the Nine, and they hunted all over China for Surefoot and the phoenix egg, but in vain. They never knew she was right under their snouts as a mouse among other mice, disguising the phoenix egg as a seed among other seeds. Those were long odds against her!"

"She hid in plain sight," Tom said.

Mr. Hu nodded. "She knew her safety lay not in brawn nor in spells but in her wits. As tiny as she was in body, there was none greater in heart, and she created the basis for the Lore and set many of the traditions for later Guardians to follow."

Tom looked from Mr. Hu to the odd band the Guardian had gathered—the somber dragon, the ape who was making faces to the delight of children in a passing tour bus, and of course the irrepressible rat who, at that moment, was trying to sell the cabby an automatic whisk broom that would clean the taxi all by itself with a push of a button. They were the tiger's friends and now they were Tom's. No, the odds weren't so bad after all.

Even so, there did not seem to be much they could do if Vatten brought the whole monstrous Clan of the Nine against them before they could take refuge among the dragons, and yet the faster they went, the sooner Mistral might die. Mr. Hu was all Tom had now. His archaeologist parents had disappeared when he was young, lost in some Southeast Asian jungle and presumed dead, and now his grandmother was gone as well.

Tom truly owed his life to the tiger. In attempting to regain the phoenix egg Tom had nearly died, and the Guardian had sacrificed some of his own life to save his apprentice. The process had left Mr. Hu dangerously weak against his enemies.

It seemed to the boy that the least he could do was to smooth the Guardian's lapels. If the tiger had one flaw, it was his vanity. "What made the Guardians leave China?"

Mr. Hu raised a hand to pat Tom's. "Wars and rebellions were tearing China apart in the 1850s, but that had happened in other centuries. Guardians have always remained outside the quarrels of humans or other creatures. Their one task is to keep the phoenix safe from everyone. They never sought refuge among the dragons or any magical creatures because others might think the Guardians were becoming their allies. I do so now only with the greatest reluctance, and it is only temporary until I recover. But fleeing to America was different. That Guardian could hide among the humans without compromising his neutrality. And we have hidden here successfully until now."

As Tom stole a glance at the tiger, he felt a twinge of guilt when he saw how wearily the Guardian slumped against the seat, keeping his eyes closed and husbanding his strength for the journey to the dragon kingdom. There was no way he could help them hold off Vatten's monsters.

"Is it very far?" Tom asked.

"Yes, even with a jet plane," Mistral said, "but we will be using other means."

Tom assumed she meant a magical spell. "Where is it then?"

"Humans know more about outer space than they do about the oceans," Mistral said. "There are many places they have never violated, and the dragon mages work powerful spells to keep it that way."

The cab rolled down the hill into the Fisherman's Wharf area, where most of the fishing boats had been chased out and the stores converted into T-shirt and souvenir stands. The area was filled with tourists. Despite the late afternoon fog coming in from the bay, they stubbornly insisted on wearing shorts as they walked between the many motels and restaurants, watched the jugglers and musicians playing on the streets, and dined by the sidewalk vendors selling crab and shrimp. Everywhere Tom looked, buildings and sidewalks were jammed, and somewhere he heard a cable-car bell clanging merrily. There wasn't a sign of trouble here either.

Eventually the taxi turned into a section that catered to those few fishermen left with shops selling rope and tackle and boat engines and even anchors. All of the shops were already shut up for the day. The cab continued on to a pier that Tom had never seen before. As Mr. Hu paid the cabby, the rest of them got out the luggage.

Everybody but the tiger was carrying something as they headed onto the pier. Even so, it worried Tom to see how the elderly tiger was shuffling along, and the others adjusted their steps to a snail's pace. On either side were two-story buildings with stores on the bottom and apartments above.

Mistral picked up her head. "Finally, civilization," the dragon murmured.

If his friend considered this civilized, Tom was beginning to have second thoughts about the dragon kingdom. All he saw were some dingy stores with signs so faded that he could not read them. No wonder it was almost deserted.

In one dusty window he saw an old hand-lettered sign that declared, ATTIRE FOR DISCRIMINATING MERPERSON. Its mannequins were all of mermen and -women.

Despite the danger, Mistral grew more and more excited as she walked along. She had lived many years in exile, and though she had been driven away by her own kind, she still took pride in her dragonhood. "Well, Tom, whatever happens to me, the sights you'll see! The marvels of the land pale in comparison with those of the sea."

"How can she think about that at a time like this?" the boy whispered to Mr. Hu.

"Let's call it a farewell tour in her imagination, if not in fact," Mr. Hu said, with a sympathetic glance at his friend.

The homesick dragon went on about dragon cuisine, telling the boy all the things he simply *must* try. Privately Tom decided to skip the raw sea slugs; there were many things that he would do for a condemned friend, but that was not one of them.

As they passed by a store with personal grooming items for the scaled, Tom couldn't help peering curiously through the window. There were neat coils of wire for fang floss, cans of polish for claws, and even dye (for removing telltale traces of silver from one's hide). Bottles of spray caught the boy's eye, because there was a sign boasting that they could solve the "problem" that dragons dared not mention. "What's the problem?" Tom whispered, pointing to the sign.

Monkey glanced at Mistral and answered in an unusually discreet low voice. "Scale lice."

Still, Mistral overheard him. "Really, some creatures have no manners," she sniffed as she walked along with a suitcase in either hand.

Fortunately the next store happened to be a gourmet shop that distracted her again. Inside were bins of dragon delicacies, such as gingered pompano candy as well as chocolate-covered swallows. Mistral peered at them hungrily. "I haven't had swallows in years."

"It's a great dragon weakness," Mr. Hu said to the puzzled boy.

Sidney, of course, sidled up to the dragon. "Why didn't you tell me before? I can get you a real good price."

Mistral, who knew the rat's tricks, raised an eyebrow. "But would they be real swallows or imitations made out of wheat gluten?"

The end of the pier was so rickety that the old boards groaned and crumbled with each step and threatened to plunge them into the bay itself at any moment. Their weight was yet another reason Tom wished they hadn't packed so many books.

The dragon led them to a dilapidated building at the very end of the pier. The wall boards had not been painted in years, and Tom could barely make out the gold letters on the sign: THE MUSEUM OF KELP. In the window hung cheap-looking plastic fishes among strips of cellophane. The building looked as ready to fall into the bay as the pier itself.

Tom turned his head to take in one last look at San Francisco, wondering if this was to be the last time. He gave a jump when he glimpsed someone with silver hair getting out of another taxi.

The tiger felt the movement. "What is it, Master Thomas?"

Tom stared around them. "I thought I saw Räv." But she was gone.

"Where?" Monkey spun around.

Mistral did not waste time searching but knocked instead at the museum door. "We have to get inside right away."

CHAPTER TWO

A moment later, a little window at the top of the door opened and an eye appeared. "We're closed." The eye narrowed sullenly. "Especially to you, outlaw."

"He saw through your disguise," a surprised Tom said to the dragon.

"He wouldn't be much of a gatekeeper if he couldn't." Mistral grunted and knocked even more loudly.

The little window banged open. "We don't want you," the gatekeeper said, "or your friends."

Mistral leaned her head near the door and said in a low voice, "You don't understand. This is the Guardian. He wishes to leave the upper realms and honor the dragons with a visit."

The eye regarded the tiger suspiciously. "He's a bit scruffy-looking, isn't he?" The gatekeeper fixed on Monkey. "And how can you even think of bringing that thief in?"

Mr. Hu glanced behind him nervously. "He is one of my escorts," he insisted to the gatekeeper.

"You could get into a great deal of trouble for pretending to be the Guardian," the gatekeeper warned.

"And you would get into a good deal more if I am who I claim to be and you refuse me entrance." Mr. Hu growled low and dangerously. "Will you take the risk?"

The eye blinked and then they heard great locks being turned inside, and the door opened. "It's your heads," the gatekeeper muttered, "especially Mistral's."

"I'll chance it," the dragon said stiffly.

The gatekeeper was a crab that came to Tom's waist and had reached the viewing window by standing on a short stepladder. Some fraying gold braid decorated the red carapace, but most of its shell was hidden by patches of purple-green moss.

As they entered, Tom could see that the door was really made of iron with planks attached to its front. He looked around at the metal walls. "This place is a fort." But to protect what?

The room was barren except for a blanket in one corner, a small television that was on, and a hot plate. Mystic signs covered every wall except the back end, which was filled from floor to ceiling by a giant tank. Perhaps at one time it had contained kelp, but it was empty now and the glass was missing.

The crab crossed its claws. "Wait here and don't touch

anything while I send a message to His Highness."

The crab scuttled sideways to a small tank that Tom had missed before. Quickly the crab picked up a stylus and drew a diagram upon the wall. Then, with its claw, the gatekeeper reached into the water and wrote on the side of the fish that waited patiently, twitching only now and then as the stylus tickled some sensitive area. Wherever the point of the stylus touched, the fish's side glowed so that soon its side was covered in a strange curly script that Tom assumed was the dragon script. "Make it quick now to the Winter Palace, and I'll see that you get a treat," the gate-keeper promised.

The next instant, the fish vanished.

"I'm surprised to hear the king is at his Winter Palace rather than his summer one," Mistral said.

The crab scuttled impatiently back to his television. "There's a lot of things that would surprise you."

"Such as?" Mistral asked.

The gatekeeper kept one eyestalk turned to the screen while the other stared at the dragon. "It would be bad enough that the Clan of the Nine raid deeper and deeper into the kingdom, but there is also a terror stalking the kingdom. No one knows where it will strike."

"So there's trouble in the sea as well as the land," Monkey murmured.

"Water is Vatten's element," Mr. Hu said. "Here he would be even stronger."

"Perhaps, perhaps not. We dragons are an ancient race, and yet there are parts of the ocean that even we do not know, and new enemies we have not met," Mistral said. "But it's curious that terror comes at a time when Vatten is rousing."

"That's not all that's strange," the gatekeeper said with a bubbly snort. "I've never seen a more suspicious lot than yours."

Mistral tried to learn more about the terror from the gatekeeper, but he seemed to have decided he had said enough and kept silent—except to tell Tom or Sidney not to touch anything whenever they fidgeted.

While the crab watched some game show on the old battered black-and-white television, the others spent an uncomfortable time until the fish suddenly appeared back in its tank. Reluctantly the crab left his show and went over to the messenger to peer at the writing. "Well," he said, scratching his shell in surprise, "it's your funerals. You're to go to the palace." He twisted his eyestalks to stare at Mistral. "Even you."

Mr. Hu and Monkey changed into their true shapes. The tiger's clothes stayed the same, for the Guardian insisted on dressing like a gentleman in all forms he took, but Monkey's transformed into a robe and cap.

Mistral's shimmering suit, on the other hand, became black scales. Self-consciously she ran a paw over her scarred, dented hide.

"I'd be ashamed to go back looking like that." The gatekeeper grunted and pointed. "Every honor and title scraped from you."

Mistral raised her head as regally as any empress. Despite her bare scales, there was a power and beauty in her lithe body. "That's my business," she said, and indicated her companions. "We'll need four breathing charms too."

Bubbles frothed around the annoyed gatekeeper's mouth. "Gassers should stay on the land where they belong." However, he rummaged around in a box by the blanket and took out four little pouches on strings, which he flung at them.

Monkey snagged them neatly and handed one to Tom. "Put this around your neck."

As Tom obeyed, Monkey hastily began stripping the hairs from his tail and converting them into little sea horses that floated in the air as if it were water.

"What are you doing now?" Tom asked.

"It's always wise to take precautions when you deal with dragons." Monkey winked as a cloud of sea horses surrounded him.

The gatekeeper sidled over to the wall to the left of the dusty tank and quickly traced a claw over one group of mystic signs as he murmured a spell. Then he twisted his eyestalks to look at them over his shoulder, gesturing impatiently. "Single file. No running. No pushing."

"Is this going to be enough?" Tom fingered the pouch around his neck doubtfully.

"You'll be able to breathe just fine," Mr. Hu assured him. "Dragon magic is one of the oldest and finest in the world."

"But," Sidney whispered helpfully to Tom, "if you want insurance, I can dig out some scuba gear."

Mr. Hu rapped the rat on top of his head before he could take his merchandise from his fur. "What my apprentice needs is confidence, not unnecessary equipment."

"No shoving, single file," the gatekeeper repeated in a bored, flat voice.

"I'll go first," Mistral announced eagerly.

The gatekeeper snapped a claw at her maliciously. "Then you'll be the first to die."

Mistral leaned forward until the gatekeeper shrank back. "I'd choose that fate over turning into a sour insect any day."

"There never was anyone who could beat a dragon for pride," Monkey said with sad admiration.

Her point made, Mistral picked up a suitcase with each forepaw. Mr. Hu had already cast a waterproofing spell on all their belongings.

"Wait for Tom on the other side of the gate," Mr. Hu called to her.

"Of course." With a nod, the dragon stepped into the tank and vanished.

Tom's mouth dropped open. "She's gone!"

"What do you expect from a gate? Hurry it up, will

you? You're keeping me from watching my favorite show," the gatekeeper snapped, tapping a foot impatiently.

Carrying his own pair of suitcases, Tom hesitated on the threshold. He had never been scared of a fight, but vanishing in thin air was something different.

Though Mr. Hu had to shuffle, he stepped beside his apprentice and offered his paw. The claws were sheathed, but Tom could see how the leather pad was scarred from the tiger's battles and adventures. "It's safer than crossing the street, Master Thomas. But if you'd feel better, we'll go together."

Tom looked up at Mr. Hu. As weak as the tiger was, Tom felt just as safe with the Guardian as he had with his grandmother. Gratefully he nodded his head.

The tiger wrapped his paw around the boy's arm. As they started forward, the gatekeeper cleared his throat noisily and held out a tin can around which he had wrapped a paper sign that read TIPS. "A gratuity would be customary," he said, shaking the can.

Mr. Hu glared at the gatekeeper. "Here's my tip for you. Learn better manners." He glanced at the boy. "Ready, Master Thomas?"

Tom nodded, and they stepped inside.

As the world seemed to vanish, the gatekeeper clacked his claws like evil castanets. "You won't be coming back. The Nameless One'll get you, and good riddance to bad rubbish!"

CHAPTER THREE

They should have reached the rear wall of the tank in a few paces, but suddenly things grew dim and shadowy, and Tom was glad the tiger was holding on to his arm.

"Just a bit more, Master Thomas," Mr. Hu said. Yet as they stepped forward, Tom felt himself surrounded by a wet, freezing darkness. A great weight was crushing his chest and limbs, and when he opened his mouth to cry out, he only took in salt water. He was drowning!

Immediately he felt Mr. Hu's forelegs around him in a strong, tight embrace. "It will be all right, Master Thomas."

Panicking, the boy dropped his suitcases as he struggled to break free. He tried to scream that he didn't want to be an apprentice anymore—he just wanted to go back to land.

Mistral seized his hands. "Don't be frightened, Tom. This will pass in a moment."

Instinctively the boy's lungs exhaled and inhaled . . . and he could breathe. It was strange. He could feel the wetness within his lungs, but it was as if he were breathing air. And he wasn't cold anymore. His eyes were also adjusting, because he could make out shapes even though it was still dark.

"What happened?" he asked.

Mistral released Tom's hands and touched the dragon charm that lay around his neck next to a protective charm Mr. Hu had given him when they had first met. "It's the magic of the charm."

Mr. Hu still held on to his apprentice as he checked him for any ill effects. "Really, Mistral," he said with worried disapproval, "the spell is so antiquated and clumsy. Master Thomas should never have experienced such difficulties. The dragon mages are far more capable than that. There are breathing spells nowadays that don't have all these horrid side effects." Satisfied that Tom was all right, he finally let go of the boy.

"The charms have never been updated because we dragons don't want many visitors," Mistral said.

"But it felt so cold and heavy too," Tom said, massaging his chest.

"You have tons of water overhead now," Mistral said, pressing her paws together in illustration. "Without magic, you could not go very deep without being crushed. And the temperatures in the deep ocean can be near freezing. It would make the floodwaters in the mansion seem like a warm bath."

"Mark this, Master Thomas. Magicians must take many things into account when they cast spells," Mr. Hu added, and motioned to his suit. "You'll notice your clothes aren't wet either."

Tom felt his own and saw that they were as dry as if he were on land. Then he looked up. "How far below are we?"

"The gate is about a mile beneath the surface on the side of the sea mount," Mistral explained. "This is the other side of the museum's tank." She gestured toward the gilded gate decorated with a continuous design of dragons biting one another's tails. They curled and twisted around the gate so that it was difficult to tell where one ended and the other began; Tom felt as if they were forming words in a script he could not read.

"What's a sea mount?" Tom asked.

"Do you think the upper realms are the only ones with high places?" Mistral asked. "What you call islands are the tips of *our* mountains." She pointed a claw at several red dots to the north and to the south. "Do you see those bits of light? They're actual volcanoes, but don't worry. The mages have placed the strongest of spells upon them so that they behave themselves." She gestured back to the smoldering mountains. "A sea mount is a volcano whose top has collapsed. But this one was knocked off in the war against Kung Kung. The legends say the floor of the sea itself was cracked in the fighting and volcanoes and mountains sprang up everywhere. And the war against Vatten will be just as bad if he has his way."

At that moment, Monkey tumbled through the gate so abruptly that he thumped into the dragon's side, dropping the suitcases he was carrying. "Oof—you need more padding."

Mistral plucked the ape from her side distastefully. "I was never meant to be a mattress for furbags."

Sidney followed a moment later. Other than a slight shiver, he didn't show any more side effects from the charm than Monkey had.

As the dragon's eyes devoured the sights hungrily, Tom saw a wistful smile spread across her face, and the boy gazed with her.

The seafloor stretched away for miles. "The sea makes me feel as small as a bug," he murmured.

"It's so vast," Mistral agreed, "that it can make even a dragon feel insignificant."

"I might have known you'd be in the company of vagabonds and thieves," a deep voice said. A dragon with an enormous plume upon his head and frilly patterns of gold and pearls decorating his muzzle and sides had been watching them. His talons were tipped in steel and armor hung on his sides. Behind him ranged another half dozen dragons equally well armed and armored, with similar patterns on their bodies.

Mistral's smile changed to a deep frown. "I see you've come up in the world, Tench, from the days when you poached my father's narwhals."

"And you've slid far below a starving poacher." Tench gestured toward Mistral's bare, scarred sides. The other dragon warriors also wore plumes, but not as large as their leader's. Tom wondered why the colored decorations on their faces looked fuzzy.

"You're to come with me. The high king wants to sentence you himself."

"From gold to steel." Mistral smiled grimly. "Why has the Royal Guard shed its parade armor for battle gear? Are you that afraid of me?"

"Considering the penalty awaiting you, it should be the other way around," Tench said smugly.

Mistral motioned with her paw. "Don't forget my friend's luggage."

"We're imperial guards, not servants," Tench snapped.

Mistral narrowed her eyes. "Don't you know who this is?" she asked as she took hold of the weakened tiger. "He is the Guardian."

The plumes of all the dragon warriors vanished, and Tom thought it was even odder that the decorations on the squad's muzzles had disappeared too, leaving only razor-edged bumps on their hides into which the plumes had retreated.

"That old cat doesn't look like he could guard a snail." Tench tried to sound brave.

Mistral simply smiled. "Do you think I would risk coming were I not in his company?"

Tench hesitated, then twisting his long neck jerked his head at his warriors and said sourly, "Take the bags."

"Don't break anything," Mistral warned as she rose upward through the water with Mr. Hu.

Leaving behind one guard, Tench and his squad surrounded them, two dragons staying close to Monkey, who kicked his way along nonchalantly. The school of sea horses trailed behind.

To Tom's surprise, the dragons' plumes slowly reappeared again. Now that he could get a closer look, he could see that the plumes were really worms who lived in tubes that followed the contours of the dragons' skulls. And the decorations on their muzzles were also alive—they were different-colored barnacles growing in patterns, and the fuzziness was created when they opened their shells and extended their tiny feathery feet. When the barnacles closed up, their edges formed hundreds of bumps that could cut.

As they swam up the steep slope of the dead volcano, Tom saw that colossal pictures several stories high had been carved into its side. The dragons truly thought on a monumental scale. In other places lava had cooled into lumps and spires and even huge disks, and these had been carved into dragons, some of them posed heroically, others looking wise. There were many strange creatures that the dragons must have met through the ages, but some were unrecognizable, for they were broken off at the waist and the pieces scattered.

Tom surveyed the ruins in shock. "Was there a battle here?"

Mistral seemed surprised as she surveyed the rubble. "No," she said slowly, pointing at the patches of wild coral that partially obscured the features of whole acres of statuary, "they could only grow that thick over time. I don't understand how it could have been neglected so badly."

"The king could use some steel wool to scrub this stuff," Sidney said, making a mental note.

Suddenly a lobsterlike creature poked its head from behind the knee of a dragon hero. Though the rocky slope at first seemed barren, Tom could now see how much sea life lived among the rocks and crevices. He also noticed small white dots swirling around.

"Does it snow in the sea?" Tom asked Mistral, holding out his hand to what he thought were snowflakes.

As she gazed at the shabby sides of the once magnificent decorations, she said absently, "No, it's old scales, bits of fish that have been eaten, and other things. When all the fish and sharks and other creatures overhead eat, some particles always fall. The creatures below depend upon that rain of food."

"Ugh," Tom said, snatching his hand back and rubbing his palm against his side.

Sidney clapped a paw over his muzzle. "You mean we're moving through someone's leftovers? Yuck!"

Tench sneered. "Gassers are fools. What do you think makes life possible in the deep ocean?" He waved a paw at the drifting particles. "The sea may look empty, but every inch is filled with some kind of life."

It made Tom a little uncomfortable to know what he was swimming through, but there was no smell to the "snow" and he soon grew used to it. They swam upward past more huge designs and monuments that covered the volcanic slopes. The dimness made the boy feel as if he were in a dream in which he was flying up the side of a giant skyscraper.

"How much farther?" Sidney puffed.

"Are your little legs getting tired?" smirked Tench.

Mr. Hu panted, "I wouldn't mind knowing too."

Tench hesitated and then dipped his head to the Guardian. "About another mile to the main gate."

"Couldn't they have put the gate in a more convenient spot?" Sidney asked.

"It's a place of great power where several lines of *ch'i* intersect," Mr. Hu explained between breaths. *Ch'i* is an energy that flows through the world like blood in a human body.

The subdued Mistral finally noticed how labored the tiger had become and said, "I think we should rest."

"His Highness ordered you to come right away." Tench glowered.

"He wants the Guardian alive," Mistral snapped.

Mr. Hu moved forward with clumsy strokes. "I'm fine."

Tom knew that the tiger was too proud to show weakness before the dragons, but the boy had no face to lose. "I'd like a rest."

Mr. Hu immediately halted. "Ah, well, if we must, Master Thomas." He seemed glad enough for a chance simply to float for a moment.

Tom requested several stops for the tiger's sake. It would have been easier to carry him, but when a worried Mistral offered, the tiger refused.

"I'll take a lift," Sidney chirped, and barely dodged Mistral's lashing tail.

"We were willing to make an exception for the Guardian, but we are not mounts for rats," she growled.

"Okay, okay," Sidney said, slipping cautiously behind Mr. Hu.

The higher they ascended, the brighter the water grew until Tom noticed a ruddy glow overhead that became steadily more brilliant.

"What's making that red light?" he asked.

Mistral's spirits picked up. "The Fire Gardens. I played

in them whenever my parents were invited to the Winter Palace."

"Are they on fire?" Tom asked, wondering how that could happen underwater.

"No, it's the light off the creatures there. You're in for a treat. Anyone who sees them always cherishes the handiwork of that great garden designer, Longwhistle." Mistral swam even faster, as if eager to forget her disappointment with the decorated slope; Tench and the others had to hurry to keep up with her.

Swimming beside the tired tiger, Tom was one of the last to reach the broad plateau that extended from the side of the mountain. What he saw made him catch his breath. Overhead, the reflection of the setting sun burned like a coal through the sea, casting a ruby net of light that spread across the darkening surface.

"Behold the Fire Gardens of Longwhistle," Mistral said with a proud wave of her paw.

"Enjoy it while you can, outlaw. It will be the last time you will see it," Tench said sourly.

"If I must die, at least I will have this," Mistral said, gazing around.

At first, Tom thought the plateau had burst into flame, but then he realized it was the flowers that grew everywhere in a thick carpet. They came in all shapes and sizes, from small globes of curled petals to explosions of red that looked like fireworks frozen forever in the sea.

If his apprenticeship brought risks like entering the ocean depths, it also brought rewards. He would never have seen this had he stayed in San Francisco. As Tom floated over to Mistral, he murmured, "It's just as beautiful as you said."

Sidney let out a whistle. "I could make a killing selling these."

Mistral, though, was looking around puzzled. "But there was always music and singing in the garden. Even the pipefish are silent."

"Wouldn't you be quiet too?" Sidney asked, and pointed up above. Overhead they saw more armored dragons swimming back and forth in formation as they drilled.

Monkey nodded. "They're outfitted for combat."

Mr. Hu watched a group training. "One would expect this sight at a frontier fort, but not within the heart of the dragon kingdom."

Monkey pirouetted gracefully in the water. "The whole place is gearing up for war."

"What's happening?" Mr. Hu asked their guards.

"You picked a fine time to visit, Guardian," Tench said. "Why do you think we don't have time to repair things? There is a terror that has destroyed troop after troop of warriors, so that our army is no longer able to keep out the invaders. Even now, our enemies raid deeper and deeper into the kingdom."

"What sort of terror?" Mr. Hu asked. Tom thought of the gatekeeper's warning.

Tench shrugged and lowered his voice. "None have survived the battle. We only know it as the Nameless One."

"I had no idea things were this bad," Mistral said.

"I'm sorry," Tom sympathized. Poor Mistral. The kingdom was no longer the lovely home she remembered.

"I smell Vatten's handiwork," Monkey said, tugging at his cap.

"I do too," the tiger murmured.

It was a more somber group that swam above the gardens. Below him, Tom saw that there were more than flowers. There were also enormous lacelike fans and vases and globes that, he was told, were sponges. Mistral pointed to a giant doily almost as large as herself. "That one was probably planted by Longwhistle." Flowers and sponges had been laid out in grand swirling designs like the writing on the gate, as if this were a secret dragon text.

Tom was startled when he saw one flower curl up in the wake of their passage. "That flower moved," he said.

When a guard laughed, Mistral glared at him and then explained. "These are all animals—anemones and worms and so on."

As they went on, Tom could see how the animals were growing over the paths. In other places they had obliterated part of the designs. Algae and barnacles were growing on the sides of the statues and benches. Everywhere were signs of neglect.

"The folks here could use a few garden tools," Sidney

muttered. The rat was taking in the sights as avidly as Tom, but in a different frame of mind: He saw a chance for profit everywhere he looked.

"They're not keeping up the gardens either," Tom whispered to Mr. Hu.

"When you're battling for your life," the tiger said grimly, "you don't think about such things as gardening."

"That's the worst," Monkey said, pointing to a building that rose from the center of the garden. It seemed to be the outline of a nautilus shell grown from living coral, but part of it had collapsed. "Was there a battle here?"

Mistral shook her head. "That's meant to be that way. It's the Folly of Uncle Tumer. It's meant to be a picturesque ruin."

"Who's Uncle Tumer? Did he build it?" Tom asked.

"No, but it's named in his honor," Mistral said as she continued to look about her. "Uncle Tumer is the greatest fool of the dragons. There are many funny legends and stories about his antics. They say he was the first court jester."

"He was the biggest idiot next to you." Tench smiled with malicious glee. "You should never have come back. You've returned in the darkest time of the dragons since the war against Kung Kung. His Highness will be in a foul mood when he sentences you."

And the other guards laughed harshly.

CHAPTER FOUR

A s they neared where the ledge met the mountainside, Tom kept looking for a palace, but all he saw was the mountain itself. He could see the top, though, and saw that it was indeed missing its peak from that war long ago. Upon the flat surface grew more gardens where strands of giant kelp waved like green hair, but there wasn't so much as a spire or tower to mark a castle.

"Where's the Winter Palace?" he asked Mr. Hu.

"The entire sea mount is the palace," the tiger explained.

Tom thought of the immense mountain. "The whole thing?"

Mistral roused herself from her thoughts. "Generations of dragons have taken thousands of years to create this masterpiece," she boasted. Even if her kingdom was under siege, a dragon could still take pride in its history. "The first levels were built by Calambac himself, the first king of the dragons." She motioned below them toward the foot of the sea mount, hidden in the darkness. "And subsequent generations added to it." She gestured proudly toward the flat top. "But the best levels were done by my clan, the Harmattanids."

Tom glanced at his friend in surprise. "Your family ruled the dragon kingdom?"

Mistral shook her head. "Really, Hu, what have you been teaching the boy?"

Mr. Hu shrugged. "We have been covering the basics he needs to survive."

"I would have thought the history of the dragons would be the most basic." Mistral sniffed, but she turned to look at Tom. "Calambac had three sons. Pangolin was the oldest, Chukar the next, and Harmattan was the youngest. In his wisdom, Calambac chose Harmattan to succeed him, and though it did not sit well with his older brothers, they agreed reluctantly. But their descendants have not always abided by Calambac's wishes and have seized the throne at different times."

"The history of the dragons is as bloody as the humans'," Monkey said.

"Well, who rules the palace now?" Tom asked.

"Langur is the king of all the dragons," Mistral said. "He's a Pangolid."

"His Highness Langur," Tench corrected.

Sidney regarded the palace in awe. "And this whole mountain is his home?"

"Yes, but as lovely as it is, it's rather quaint, isn't it?" Mistral shrugged apologetically. "But then the king doesn't do as much entertaining in the winters. Now the Summer Palace is truly grand."

If the dragon considered the Winter Palace small, Tom wondered just how large the Summer Palace was.

"If it were not for the Guardian," Tench said haughtily, "you would be entering the dungeons and not the court-room."

As Tom drew closer to the mountain's side, he could see that the ancient palace was in the same sad neglect as the Fire Gardens. Here, where life could grow, it had been allowed to cover the palace's designs until they were barely recognizable, and the statues were hidden by layers of brightly colored coral worms that looked disconcertingly like flesh. In some spots, where the rock could be seen, the faces and statues were missing noses and even limbs. As magnificent as the upper Winter Palace was, it had become as shabby as the lower slopes.

Mistral whirled around in a swirl of bubbles. "Even if you were at war, how could you let such a shameful thing happen?" she demanded in an anguished voice.

Tench bristled with every worm and barnacle. "Don't lecture us about shame, outlaw. While you were hiding safe upon the upper realms, we have been fighting for our lives."

As they approached the gates, Tom felt a tingling at the back of his neck. His first thought was that Monkey or Sidney was tickling him, but the rat was gazing in awe at the palace; and even though the ape was trying to pretend indifference, he was also studying the mountain, with the professional eye of a thief.

When Tom began to rub his neck, Mr. Hu murmured to his apprentice, "Don't fidget, Master Thomas."

"I feel something," the boy said.

Mr. Hu nodded approvingly. "You're learning to pay attention to your sensations. There is a vast channel of *ch'i* here. All my fur feels as if it's bristling, but you'll get used to that."

"You said several lines of power intersected at the gate," Tom said, lowering his hand. "Why didn't I notice it there?"

"You were too busy trying to breathe," Mr. Hu said with a kindly pat.

The main gate was huge—twenty dragons could have swum through it side by side. It was carved in the shape of a fanged mouth, but it was so overgrown with coral that Tom could not recognize it and asked Mistral what creature it was as they passed within.

"It's supposed to be Calambac himself," Mistral said, with another shake of her head. "How could they let it go like this?"

The hallway had been kept reasonably clean and the

walls were filled with trophies from the dragons' many wars. There were giant war axes and swords and spears and many more weapons with odd-shaped blades that looked so heavy, no human could have swung them. Captured war banners, some of them so old they were hardly more than tattered ribbons, hung from the ceiling, and busts of savage creatures stood in niches. At least, Tom hoped they were statues and not preserved heads.

Light was cast by fish that had large glowing globes dangling from stalks on their foreheads. Because the fish swam about, the shadows shifted constantly, making the heads seem to blink.

Sidney fingered a silken banner. "I wonder how much this costs."

"Your head." Tench glowered. "If you touch another thing."

Sidney clapped his paws together with a squeal. "You know what you folks need for visitors? A gross of disposable gloves." He began to search through his fur eagerly.

"Sidney, not now," Mr. Hu said. Tom went over and grabbed the rat, so the tiger could save his strength.

"You're interrupting a deal," Sidney protested.

Tom held on to the squirming rat. "I'm saving your life," he said as he dragged the struggling rat back to the Guardian.

Tench brought them to a massive doorway some fifty feet high and a hundred feet wide. Its giant golden doors inscribed with scenes of dragon triumphs were closed. A butler fish stalked over to them on two sticklike fins from its belly. Its gills were so frilly that they seemed like a collar, and its lips extended forward to form a tiny pouting mouth.

"We must check your length," the butler said stiffly, approaching Mistral.

"What is he doing?" Tom asked Mr. Hu.

"Each rank of dragons is allowed a certain length of body," Mr. Hu explained softly to his apprentice. "The more noble the dragon, the longer he or she can be."

Despite her impending doom, Mistral could not help smiling darkly. "We dragons have a law for everything."

Apparently she met the legal requirements because the butler stepped back. "You may enter the audience chamber."

"If your father could see you now." Tench smirked and stepped through the doorway.

Mistral raised her head. "He would see that his daughter is not afraid of dying."

"I will do my best to protect you," Mr. Hu vowed.

"I knew what could happen," Mistral said, then marched with great dignity inside the great room. As he watched his friend walk toward her death, Tom remembered what Monkey had said: There never was anyone who could match a dragon for pride. He couldn't help thinking no one else could be as grand as his friend at that moment.

As they followed her, a fanfare thundered throughout

the chamber. The Guardian stood as stunned as Tom and the others.

On either side of the great doorway were balloon-shaped blue squid with fins on the sides of their heads like elephant ears. In their tentacles were conch shells and long trumpets some six feet long raised on high. The trumpets did not have the gleam of brass but seemed to be paper-thin shells shaped like tubes that flared at the mouth. There were even sousaphone-like instruments made from giant nautilus shells.

Strange fish swam overhead. They looked like sea horses that had been ironed into straight daggers, and they were covered all over with frills and striped with gaudy rainbow colors. From their thin long mouths came a merry whistling sound.

"So there are still a few pipefish left," Mistral said, pleased.

Everywhere in the chamber dragon courtiers were bending their heads or curtsying to them. Many were in war gear, so it seemed even the heart of the palace was not safe from fear of the Nameless One.

The courtiers were all of different lengths—Tom still didn't know what the specific ranks were—and their muzzles and limbs were decorated with different patterns of colored pearls, barnacles, and feathery worms. The dragon hosts were a riot of brilliant hues, as if a rainbow had shattered and fallen on their bodies; armed for war, they looked like the most magnificent and terrible creatures in the world. Mistral's bare scales stood in stark contrast to the assembly, a conspicuous symbol of her shame. Yet to Tom her pride was more than enough to clothe her.

Upon a dais at the far end of the chamber rose the largest dragon of all, with a huge pearl upon his forehead. His scales rasping against his throne, he towered over everyone, his voice booming against the vaulted ceiling. "Welcome, welcome and thrice welcome, Guardian." The king of all the dragons held out his paws. "Come forward, all of you. Or we'll make ourselves hoarse with all the shouting."

Mr. Hu almost stumbled, and Tom hurried to his side to escort him.

"Monkey, try to keep out of sight behind me as much as you can," Mr. Hu whispered as they continued on. Already they could hear murmurs from the courtiers when they saw the ape, and even more when they recognized Mistral.

The chamber was as big as an airport, with curving sides that spiraled upward to form a distant peak. As pale and fine as marble, the walls were decorated with gilt swirls and curls. As they crossed the vast floor, the pipefish danced overhead, playing their own merry greeting.

It took a while to reach the dais of living coral so black that it seemed like a lump of night sky. From within, worms

46

extended star-shaped mouths that seemed to glitter like gold.

Upon the dais, the giant Dragon King waited, his emerald scales outlined in gold with magnificent yellow plumes rising from his skull and along his spine. He alone had yellow patterns of barnacles and worms decorating his scales; however, the king's claws were tipped with steel, as if even he had to be ready for war.

The guards parted to either side while Mr. Hu and his companions prostrated themselves. As he lowered himself to the floor, the tired tiger muttered to his apprentice, "After that walk, I'm rather glad of the rest."

At a wave of the king's paw, the pipefish vanished abruptly. "And why have you decided to grace us with your presence?" the king asked.

Briefly Mr. Hu explained about Vatten's theft of the phoenix egg, their daring attempts to regain it, first getting out of an ambush and trap in a mansion and then fighting their way into the heart of his underground lair. "Though we recovered the phoenix egg, my apprentice here was injured. The only way to heal him was to seek out the Empress herself. But the spell has left me temporarily weak."

No one ever referred to that ruler of ancient China by name, though Tom now knew it was Nü Kua. Powerful and yet whimsical, she lived in a special chamber beyond time and space. At the thought of her, Tom had to control a shiver. Though he had been unconscious during the ordeal, everything he heard about her made him want to avoid her. However, the others told him she had claimed that there was a link between them and that she would see him again.

There was a murmur of surprise from the court, and the king rose upon his dais. "I've never heard of such a thing. No one has seen the Empress for thousands of years."

"She left the mark of her favor upon my apprentice," Mr. Hu explained.

"Rise, boy. Show me," said the king, gesturing.

Tom glanced around all the dragons, aware of how they were craning their necks to see him better. The king loomed over him like a small hill.

"Go on, Master Thomas," Mr. Hu urged. "Don't keep His Highness waiting."

Tom rose shakily to his feet. He'd almost forgotten the golden scale from her gown. She'd pressed it on his cheek before they had left.

"Let me examine it," the king commanded in a thunderous voice and held out a great paw that could have swatted Tom like a fly.

Trembling, Tom tried to take it off his cheek but it wouldn't budge. "It's like it's glued," he said.

The king motioned to a dragon in an emerald collar with matching plume worms down his spine and intricate black-and-gold patterns decorating his scales. "Grand Mage, fetch it."

The Grand Mage was so old that he shuffled forward, his stomach brushing the floor. When he tried to pull off the scale, he gave a cry and stepped back, wringing his paw as if he had just been shocked. "It's protected by powerful magic," he said in a voice that creaked like old leather. "Perhaps the tale is true."

The king clasped his paws together and closed his eyes as he thought for a moment. When he opened them again, he smiled. "Of course, it must be true. Would the Guardian lie?"

"To save my apprentice, I gave him some of my life force," Mr. Hu said. "I hope to rest here until I recover enough strength to defend the egg against Vatten on my own. Until then, I must depend upon your power. I won't trouble you for long."

"Nonsense." The king spread his paws wide in delight. "Stay as long as you like, though we fear we cannot show all the hospitality we should. Where is my healer?"

Another elderly dragon stepped forward. Unlike the others, she wore no armor, only a silver collar around her neck that almost matched the color of her scales. Glowing coral worms decorated her hide in intricate spiral patterns of red and blue barnacles and mussels. And her eyes were filled with a warm kindness.

"Here, Your Majesty," she said with a respectful curtsy.

The king waved a paw. "Attend the Guardian. Treat him with all the care you would give me."

"As you wish," the healer said, curtsying again.

The king leaned forward eagerly. "And the phoenix egg. Do you have it?"

Mr. Hu hesitated, then drew the pouch from around his neck and opened it. As the assembled dragons watched with hushed breath, the Guardian reverently drew out the phoenix egg and lifted it in both paws. There were far more impressive carvings on the palace and more magnificent jewelry on the dragons than the phoenix egg, which was currently in disguise as a coral rose. And there were not a few doubtful glances at the ordinary-looking rose until suddenly, as if in answer to the tiger's touch, Tom saw a flash of red fire.

With a gasp, the assembled dragons bowed their heads, even the Dragon King.

When he lifted his head again, the king wrapped his tail around his throne and gripped it with his hind paws as he leaned forward all the better to gaze at the stone flower.

"Would that the world could be at peace and the phoenix could be reborn," he wished fervently, gazing at it with such a desperate hunger that it made Tom feel uneasy.

Mr. Hu must have felt something similar, because he lowered it and instantly the rose petals grew as dull and ordinary as usual. He put the egg away in the pouch and hid it inside his clothes. "I think that is the wish of all creatures of goodwill, but he may not while there is any creature of ill will who could misuse him."

The Dragon King settled back upon his throne, coil after coil. "And yet there needn't be any creatures of ill will if he were awake."

"That is the paradox of the phoenix, isn't it?" Mr. Hu said gently. "He cannot be born until there is peace."

"And there are many who would say we cannot have peace until he is born," the Dragon King said, brooding for a moment. "Such a priceless treasure must be kept safe in our vault."

Mr. Hu dipped his head diplomatically. "I'm afraid the egg must remain with me, Your Highness."

The king's eyes narrowed. "If I did not know any better, I would say you don't trust us. Why did you come to us then?"

"I mean no disrespect to Your Highness," Mr. Hu said with a deep bow. "But unfortunately even the noblest hearts have been corrupted by the phoenix's power." He looked to the Grand Mage for confirmation.

The elderly dragon gave an uncomfortable cough. "The Lore is full of such tales, Your Highness."

Mr. Hu touched his forehead almost to the floor again. "Of course, I would never suspect Your Highness."

"It would be wise not to," the king said stiffly.

"But please indulge me," Mr. Hu said, still looking down humbly. "I will sleep easier if it is with me."

The king glared at the tiger, for it was obvious he was not used to being refused anything. Tom expected all of them to be dumped into the deepest dungeon, but then the king's mouth composed itself into a sly smile. "How can I refuse anything to the Guardian? So be it."

Having gained this much, Mr. Hu decided to risk even more. With his face still to the floor, he said, "Your Majesty, if I may mention, Monkey is also in my party. If I give my pledge for his good behavior, may he also stay?"

The request taxed even the king's goodwill, and he drummed his claws upon his throne, glancing at some gilded dragons who seemed to be his counselors. They held a whispered conversation among themselves and when the king swung his head over toward them, they whispered in his ear. Finally he turned back to the Guardian with a forced smile. "Do I have his oath as well?"

"Certainly, absolutely, positively, Your Royal Highness," Monkey said, bowing earnestly several times. "How could I refuse such a wise and powerful potentate? I promise my good behavior. I swear on behalf of every part of me that stands before you."

They heard a faint jingling sound as a small dragon crept around the dais. The mouths of many yardlong, rainbow-colored fish were attached like leeches to his head, and his tail was covered with hundreds of little bells.

"Be careful what you swear, ape," the creature said,

and draped himself casually over the steps of the dais. Neither the king nor the rest of his court seemed upset by such familiarity. "For you may have a short memory, but Heaven has a long one and will remember your oath."

"Who's he?" Tom asked Mr. Hu.

The tiger lifted his head. "The court jester," he whispered back.

"I only want to help the Guardian," Monkey said, "and if that means I must swear to be a perfect guest, then so be it."

"A guest must be perfect with an imperfect host." The jester shook his tail at the king.

The king leaned over to warn, "And how am I imperfect, Uncle Tumer? Don't I put up with your insults?"

Tom remembered the purposeful ruin in the garden. "Is that the same Uncle Tumer the Folly was named for?" Tom asked Mr. Hu softly. "He looks awfully young."

"No, there is only one court jester at a time, but each one adopts the name of Uncle Tumer," the tiger said.

The jester shook his head this time so that the ribbonfish flew all about. "A perfect host would demand a perfect wit, whereas an imperfect host will put up with my imperfect skills. And so you suit me."

There was dead silence in the court for a moment, and then the king sat back on his dais with a chuckle. "Quite true, Fool."

When they were sure it was safe, the rest of the court

laughed and the Fool flopped on his back as if he were sunning himself on a beach.

"How can he get away with something like that?" Tom wondered.

"The king's fool has license where everyone else"— Mr. Hu nodded toward Mistral—"does not."

Scuttling on all fours like a beetle, Sidney edged in. "Don't forget me, Mr. H."

When the laughter had subsided, Mr. Hu gestured to the rat. "I also have another . . . um . . . companion. Sidney," Mr. Hu said.

Unable to resist making a deal, the rat popped up. "I can give you a nice deal on some polish for your dais."

"Not now, Sidney," Tom said, dragging the rat back down on the floor and holding him there.

Everyone held his breath, waiting to see the king's reaction, but fortunately he appeared to be in a good mood. "You have the most interesting acquaintances, Guardian," he said, lacing his claws together. "Why don't you speak to my steward, furry one?"

Despite Tom's best efforts, Sidney raised a paw. "Hey, steward, whoever you are, see me afterwards, okay?"

Mr. Hu cleared his throat. "Your Highness, if I may mention, the outlaw Mistral is also in my company. Would the same protection extend to her?"

"Perhaps she should ask me herself," the king suggested.

Mistral raised her head defiantly. "I've never been one to beg."

There was a gasp from the court, and the king coiled himself on his dais. "You were always the proud one, Cousin." The king paused. "But then we are of the same royal blood. I was wrong to lose my temper when last we met and have regretted it since. And in these perilous times, I need a mighty warrior like you. You've been away far too long . . . Your Grace," he added.

All around them, the water was filled with astonished murmurs.

The king pantomimed setting something down. "I bestow upon you the Duchy of the Flaming Hills."

"Your Highness, I don't know what to say," Mistral said, bowing her head sincerely. With just a few words, the king had transformed her from outlaw to duchess.

"That would be a first," the king said with a droll laugh as he gestured to his chamberlain.

With great ceremony, the chamberlain stepped forward and dipped his long neck. "According to the law, you are allowed an extra two meters, Your Grace."

"Yes, of course," the stunned dragon said. It took her only a moment for her body to grow the permitted extra length. When she had, the dragons stamped their paws so that the floor shook as if in an earthquake.

Resting his chin on a paw, the king regarded his fool. "Uncle Tumer, do you still think I am an imperfect host?"

The Fool moved forward on all fours with his belly low like a stalking cat and winked at the new duchess as he announced to the king, "Your only perfection is your foolishness."

Mistral suddenly gaped. "Ring Neck, is that you?"

The Fool raised his tail and wriggled it so that the hundreds of little bells rang. "Who is this Ring Neck? I'm Uncle Tumer, for I've earned the name well."

Tom wondered if the Fool had gotten the other name because of the band of lighter scales that ran around his neck.

The king's brows had drawn together and Tom held his breath, waiting for the storm, but the angry mood gave way to curiosity. "You should be honored, Fool, to be in my royal presence."

The Fool wagged his head, and the attached fish again flew like ribbons. "But you are a fool by nature while I am a fool by effort."

"He's going to lose his head for sure," Tom whispered to the ape.

"He won't lose his head," Monkey said. "Condemned dragons are skinned alive."

"That would apply equally to apes who misbehave," Mr. Hu warned.

Upon his dais, the king raised his head haughtily. "Have a care, Fool, or I might become the perfect host and demand a perfect fool."

"But then I would also be safe," the Fool said, "for what perfect host would want a fool without a perfect skin? And what host could be perfect without a sense of humor?"

The king clutched the dais so tightly that Tom thought his claws would gouge holes into the coral. "True," he admitted finally, "but one day you will go too far."

"That fool dances a fine line," Monkey whispered. "I wonder why."

"Too far one way or the other and he'll break his neck," Tom agreed. "He's like a tightrope walker."

"As are we all," Mr. Hu murmured.

CHAPTER FIVE

After the king left his throne, it was hard to say who was in need of more help—the exhausted tiger or the dazed dragon, now the ruler of the Duchy of the Flaming Hills. All the courtiers had made a point of converging on Mistral to congratulate the high king's new favorite.

"Better get out of the way," Monkey said, tugging at Tom's sleeve, "or you'll get trampled."

"You don't need to tell me twice," Tom said, ducking as a dragon with blue scales swam overhead, tail whipping.

As Tom and Sidney guided Mr. Hu over to the side, the boy observed to the tiger, "I thought I saw something in the rose. It was like a spark of fire."

"Ah, so you noticed," Mr. Hu observed with pleasure. "Not everyone can. The training must be sharpening your senses."

They stood near a column, almost forgotten—except for the occasional hostile glance shot at Monkey by the dragons.

"Have you ever thought of returning the staff you stole?" Tom asked Monkey, who was doing his best to hide behind the others.

"They weren't using it." The ape shrugged defensively.

Having seen the ape in action with the staff, Tom knew how much the staff was a part of Monkey, like his paw—or his mouth, which could do almost as much damage as the staff.

The audience with the king seemed to have used up all of Mr. Hu's energy. Now that everyone's eyes were off him, he leaned heavily on Tom and Sidney. "I'm glad to see Mistral finally getting her due," he said.

Even Monkey had to agree. "That overgrown lizard's had a hard enough life."

Tom watched with satisfaction as scaled, glittering nobles and officials swirled around and over Mistral's head like a cloud of fireflies, trying to catch her attention. After all their adventures he had come to think of her as a friend, and he knew what it meant for her to end her lonely exile.

Mistral, for her part, simply murmured her thanks, still stunned at the turn in her fortunes.

From the increasing pressure on his shoulder, Tom could tell the Guardian was weakening and he tried signaling to the dragon.

"Stop it," Mr. Hu growled as his apprentice pointed meaningfully at the exhausted Guardian. "Let Mistral have her moment."

However, it was the new duchess who bowed her head in apology when she saw Tom's signal. "If you'll excuse me, I'd like to settle the Guardian and my companions."

A dragon with an emerald hung around his throat regarded Tom with annoyance but was all smiles for Mistral. "Yes, of course, Your Grace, but then we really must talk. If you would just put a word in for me with His Highness—"

"Balderdash," said a dragon with a swish of her tail, the rubies and pearls of her tail ring flashing in the light of the floating lanterns. "There's a good reason no one will listen to you, but *I* have an idea—"

"Yes, I want to hear all your suggestions," Mistral said. She knew what to do when faced with a horde of monsters but seemed quite at a loss with the courtiers. Apologizing and promising to listen, she waded through the eager group to join Mr. Hu.

Now that he had seen which way the winds were blowing, Tench took the opportunity to swim up to her and bow his head. "I'm glad that things have worked out for you, Your Grace."

"I'm sure," Mistral said.

"I hope you didn't misinterpret my little charade," Tench said in a low voice. "I was only acting hostile because

I fear there's a spy in my squad. Actually, I have always wished the best for you."

"You are a very good actor indeed." Mistral grunted. "Now if you'll excuse me."

"Of course," Tench said.

A bright yellow sea slug as large as Tom's head swam up to them. The orange-and-red frills along its spine flattened as it dipped its head. "Your Grace, this way to your apartments."

The officious slug swam with sharp undulations of its body as it led them through a side door and down a hallway. Tom noticed that a guard followed closely on Monkey's heels.

As they swam down a corridor, Mistral asked, "And what of my branch of my clan?"

"They do as well as any in these times," the servant said sympathetically. "Savage raiders trouble us all. And there is the Nameless One. No one returns from fighting it." The servant's frills quivered all over with fear.

Mistral sucked in her breath sharply. "A bad time to come indeed," she said, paraphrasing Tench's words. "I would like to send word to them to find out how they are faring."

"As you wish, Your Grace," the servant said, bending in acknowledgment.

They came to a large doorway that opened on a huge channel that seemed to run from the bottom of the palace to the very top. Creatures on the walls gave off a soft glow as Tom stared down. The wide tube seemed to go on forever, its lower levels lost to view, as if it had no bottom at all. Even though he knew he was hovering in one place, looking down at the vastness made him feel as if he were falling. "How far does this reach?"

The sea slug swam closer and fluttered its frills confidentially. "I'm not sure, but rumors say that it goes past the seafloor to the very center of the earth, and it's said that the oddest things sometimes find their way up into the palace."

Sidney drifted in closer to Monkey, who also stared down into the darkness. "Like what?" he asked nervously.

The servant's frills rippled as though it enjoyed sharing the rumors. "Like ghosts from the time the world was born. Or monsters that were better left in the shadows."

"Have you ever seen any?" Mistral demanded.

"Well, no," the servant admitted.

"Then let's have no servants' gossip," Mistral scolded. "You'll scare the boy."

"And the rat too," Sidney said, bumping into Monkey as he tried to stay near.

The servant dipped its head in deference to Mistral but said, "After thousands of years, Your Grace, who knows what tale might become true if people believe it long enough? And I will state one unassailable fact: The Winter Palace has taken on a life of its own. In the lower levels, tube worms and barnacles and sponges have taken over many of the corridors and reshaped them so that they no longer correspond to the ancient maps. If the palace itself can grow and change, why can't stranger things happen within?"

Hovering within the channel, Tom could almost hear the palace murmuring to itself. It seemed as if they were swimming inside a live mammoth creature.

Looking up, he thought the channel seemed just as endless, though he knew it could not be. At each story was a ring of doorways for that level, all of them intricately carved, but the details were lost under layers of lichen or coral worms or barnacles.

"If you wouldn't mind, I would like to rest," Mr. Hu said weakly.

"Yes, of course," the servant said, and immediately began to undulate upward.

Mr. Hu was going to try to swim after their guide, but Tom called out, "How far is it to our rooms?"

Mistral understood immediately. "I'll carry him."

"I'm not a baby," Mr. Hu protested. Even so, he seemed glad when his friend cradled him carefully.

They went past level after level of rooms until they came to the upper floors where the living quarters were. Here the hallways and rooms were on a more personal scale for dragons, but they were still huge for Tom and his friends.

There was a fairylike effect to the walls and ceilings where the lava had petrified into folds and flower petal–like shapes. The glowing jellyfish floated like colored paper lanterns with rainbow ribbons hanging from the bottoms.

"Careful of the tentacles," Monkey warned, waving his paw and creating a current to send one jellyfish drifting to the side. "Dragons don't feel the sting, but we will."

Mistral had a suite of rooms with a large window overlooking the Fire Gardens. Decorating the walls were floor-length tapestries of scenes with dragons.

Now that she had been welcomed back, Mistral seemed to have shed years and took pride in pointing to one scene showing a dragon tearing at a volcano with his claws as lava erupted around him and great clouds of steam rose through the water. "That's Samiel, daughter of Harmattan, who saved the dragons by diverting a lava flow against our enemies." She paused briefly by another tapestry that displayed a proud dragon rising on his hind paws as monsters surrounded him. "And that's my ancestor Kamsin. When a great horde of our enemies attacked the kingdom, he went to meet them. The Pangolids were late to join him—some say deliberately. When his entire army was dead, he used all of his magic to destroy the invaders and himself as well."

"Why didn't he do that in the first place?" Tom asked.

"Because it created such devastation that the area has never recovered to this day," Mistral said.

The tapestries appeared to vibrate and seethe, and Tom assumed they were made from living things like so much of the dragon kingdom. Curious, he examined them closer and saw that the pictures were formed by tiny fleshy spikes sticking out from the backs of worms.

When Mistral saw him examining them, she explained helpfully, "Those are made from specially bred nudibranchs."

The others were assigned rooms less grand than Mistral's but still huge by any standard. Monkey's, though, was the only one without a window. "So there's only one way out of my room," he observed dryly.

"And there will be a servant in attendance just outside," the sea slug said smoothly.

Tom noted that the servant was a dragon with the steel-tipped claws of a warrior, and his livery design was painted with some kind of glowing paint rather than true barnacles. He wondered if their "servant" had been hastily recruited from the Royal Guard rather than the palace staff.

When they finally put Mr. Hu in his bed, it brought up another problem, because as luxurious as the palace was, dragon furniture was designed for supporting great weights rather than for comfort. The bed and chaise lounges were no more than ledges.

"We'll need some sort of cushions for our guests," Mistral said.

"I'll have some fabric stuffed with the softest kelp right

away," the sea slug said, and fluttered away.

The new duchess was in fine form as she oversaw the accommodations for her friends—even, as she noted, for the furbag of an ape. They soon had Mr. Hu settled on a newly made mattress and pillow, with others being made for Tom, Sidney, and Monkey. The elderly tiger was grateful to be able to lie down.

Monkey had settled in a corner of the Guardian's room. If he was upset by his treatment, he pretended not to care.

When a small stone table was placed next to his bed, Mr. Hu took the pouch from his neck and carefully drew out the phoenix egg and placed it upon the tabletop where he could see it. Tom saw the flash of fire once again for a moment before it grew dull. At Mistral's command, a lounge with new cushions was placed near the table, for one of them would be keeping watch while the Guardian rested.

When the Grand Mage entered and asked Mr. Hu one last time if he would not feel safer putting the phoenix egg in the vault, the tiger refused politely. "But if I may ask a favor, I would like my apprentice to continue learning the Lore." The tiger motioned to their suitcases, which had already been brought to his room. "I didn't have time to write a lesson plan, but I'll do one after a nap. Would you be so kind as to take over his studies for a while?"

The Grand Mage eyed Tom as if he had his doubts about having a human as a student. "I'll do what I can."

By the time Mr. Hu had changed to a sleeping gown, the dragon healer had also arrived. "Now let's see what's the problem, shall we?" she said in the bedside manner of all doctors.

As Mr. Hu explained that the Empress had helped him share some of his blood and soul with his apprentice, she nodded her head. "Fascinating. Amazing. Did she really?" When she was done examining the Guardian, she smiled. "What you need to do is rest. Your own body will replenish your energy."

"Healer, since this matter involves magic, perhaps you should also consult me," the Grand Mage said.

Stepping to the side, the two held a whispered but heated discussion. Finally the healer dipped her head. "Yes, perhaps that would be best."

"What would be best?" Mr. Hu demanded.

"Sleep will speed the healing process," the Grand Mage said quickly, and glanced at the healer. "Won't it?"

"It can do that," the healer said, but she looked troubled.

"Is something wrong, healer?" Mistral asked.

"I've had word that my clan's lands were raided the other day," the healer said hastily, and she sent her assistant from the room.

"It's all too common news nowadays." The Grand Mage sighed.

The healer insisted on examining Tom as well. "As far

as I can tell, the boy seems better than fine."

"He and the tiger are of one blood now," Mistral said.

"I daresay he's the proof of that." The healer used a claw to scratch notes on a lichen-covered tablet.

By then, her assistant had returned with a small golden box. Opening the lid, the healer used a silken handkerchief to lift out a baseball-sized stone that shone white like a small moon. "This should be about right for the tiger's weight."

Mistral frowned. "That's quite a bit of dream stone."

The rat leaned forward enviously. "Do you know what a rock that size costs on the topside?" he whispered to Tom.

The Grand Mage dipped his head politely. "It's necessary to help the patient sleep. Isn't it, healer?"

The healer hesitated and then nodded. "Yes, most certainly." Holding it as carefully as if it were a diamond, she placed it in the tiger's paw. "Now rest and heal."

"Yes, rest. That would be nice." Mr. Hu closed his eyes, already drowsy. Even now, though, the Guardian could not resist murmuring instructions to his apprentice. "While I am incapacitated, you will stand in my stead on matters of the phoenix. I know this is a great burden to place on such young shoulders, but I have every confidence in you."

With a gulp, Tom glanced at the innocent-looking rose upon the table. "But I haven't been your apprentice very long. Ask Mistral or Monkey instead."

The amber eyes that had grown dull flared briefly into life again. "Neither of them is my apprentice."

Tom shook his head. "Pick someone else. I can't do it."

"Are you saying there is something wrong with my judgment?" Mr. Hu demanded.

"No," the boy said quickly. "I'm just saying there's something wrong with me. All I've ever done is get into trouble."

"All your life, your teachers and your schoolmates and your neighbors have been telling you you're worthless until you've believed them. But you must judge yourself not by others' opinion but by what is inside you," Mr. Hu said sternly. "Not only do you have a great heart, but you have Mistress Lee's blood . . . and mine now as well."

"Hu's right," Mistral said gently. "Even when the other dragons treated me like pond scum, I knew I was more than that."

"And look at the old girl now," Sidney coaxed. "She's a duchess."

Tom realized he was surrounded by his friends and the might of the dragon kingdom. Surely the egg was safe enough. What decisions would he need to make before Mr. Hu was up and around again? "I'll try."

Mr. Hu regarded him from under drooping eyelids. "And when you don't trust your eyes, trust your nose, Master Thomas. Not everything is as it appears." As he slipped into sleep, the orders became more mixed, including a command to wash his hands thoroughly before eating. Finally Mr. Hu fell silent as he came under the spell of the dream stone.

Tom watched the tiger's chest rise and fall as he slept. He'd been uncomfortable with the tiger at first, but he'd come to realize that Mr. Hu cared about him as much as he did about the phoenix egg. Without the tiger prowling about and telling him what to do, he felt lost, and yet he was now the interim Guardian.

"You are safe here for as long as you need," Mistral promised her slumbering friend, "and we will keep guard."

From the bed, the tiger gave a deep purr like the rumbling of a truck.

"I think he's having sweet dreams," Monkey said.

As the other dragons withdrew, Mistral sank down on the floor. "I feel like I'm in a dream myself."

Monkey could not resist teasing her as he restored the little apes to his tail. Their sea horse disguises had worked perfectly because no one had paid them any attention in the throne room or when they had slipped into the room. "Duchesses don't sit like sacks of potatoes."

"Well, this duchess does," Mistral said. "This morning I was an outlaw expecting to die, and tonight I have honors and titles. What a turn of fortune."

The rat, who had managed to control his instincts up to now, sidled over. "You're going to be needing some help furnishing your palace."

Mistral placed a paw to her forehead, looking dazed again. "I hadn't thought about that. And there'll be servants with the palaces. And my lands will have people. My father took care of everything. Now I'll have to do that."

Tom started to reach a hand out to pat his friend's shoulder reassuringly but hesitated. She was a duchess now, and perhaps she wouldn't welcome any familiarities. "You'll make a good ruler," he said instead.

"And you'll make a good Guardian," Mistral said. The new noble lady had no qualms about her dignity with her friends and rested a paw upon the boy's shoulder. "As soon as Hu is well, we'll travel to my new home together." Then she rose. "It must be evening now. It's time for the star rise."

"Do you mean shooting stars?" Tom asked, thinking of falling meteors.

"I mean what I say," Mistral boasted. "The night sky is nothing compared to the evening sea, where the stars are all alive." Stepping to a curtain, she drew it back from the tall window. Below they could see the Fire Gardens shining red and yellow like a bed of coals in the black water. "The gardens are beautiful by day, but Longwhistle designed it to be its loveliest when the creatures wake at night and give off their light."

Monkey pressed his nose against the glass. "I'll memorize the view for when I'm in my room staring at the four walls."

Then, as Tom watched, it seemed like thousands and thousands of stars were rising from the abyss below the sea mount toward the blackness above.

"Those stars are tiny creatures rising to feed on the plankton on the surface," Mistral explained. "They swim upward when the darkness gives them more protection, and larger and larger animals follow to feed on them. Many creatures can give off light. Some use it to communicate or to fool their enemies or to find prey. But the waters around the sea mount are especially rich because sea currents rise upward against the mount's side and bring up the nutrients that sustain many plankton, and *that* supports all the other creatures in turn."

"I'd rather think of them as stars," Tom said, picturing them bursting out of the water and into the night sky itself.

"But the star rise is millions of hunters seeking even more prey," Mistral murmured dreamily. "It's hard to believe that such a lovely spectacle can hide so many life-and-death dramas."

Tom watched more and more of the lights climb past the mount until they seemed like luminous clouds, trailing ribbons that twisted as if in a dancer's hands. Sometimes there were bursts of light like fireworks or streaks of lightning. Others flashed steadily like neon signs or rippled like fire.

Tom turned to look at his dragon friend. She'd suffered great loneliness and many hardships, but as the light from the rising "stars" reflected faintly over her face, he knew she belonged in the dragon kingdom. "Welcome home, Your Grace," he said softly.

•

CHAPTER SIX

I nspired by Mistral's example, Tom set to work to make himself into someone worthy of being a Guardian. He'd never been a great student before, either in school or with his grandmother's magical lessons, but he threw himself into his studies now with the Grand Mage. Though the scholarly dragon had been reluctant to take on a human pupil, he proved to be a conscientious tutor.

They met in the Grand Mage's chambers amid scroll-filled shelves, some covered with colonies of barnacles. Except for the table and benches, the only other furnishing was a large mirror that always appeared to reflect an empty room. There, perched upon cushions to bring him up to the table height, Tom applied himself.

Mr. Hu hadn't been awake long enough to prepare a study guide with the Grand Mage, so the elderly dragon wound up teaching him Dragon Lore instead—which meant, among many other things, Tom also had to learn the serpentine, curling runes that the ancient dragons had used. There were nearly four times as many symbols as in the English alphabet, and some of them corresponded to syllables that hurt the boy's throat when he tried to pronounce them. Others made the back of his neck tingle, as if there were a power sleeping within the curving lines.

Unfortunately, despite Tom's intentions, he found parts of Dragon Lore drearily dull—did he really have to learn about Calambac V's moss collection? (At least he was able to talk the Grand Mage out of a field trip down to the lower levels to see it, for the dragons never seemed to throw away anything and had preserved it these thousand years.)

When he was fighting yawns or getting a headache over an equation, Tom began again to regret becoming Mr. Hu's apprentice—especially since every day seemed to bring news of destruction by the Nameless One or of more raids by Vatten's monsters.

And yet as trouble mounted around him, there was also part of the boy that welcomed the normalcy of classes—just as there was a part of him that insisted he had to keep his word to Mr. Hu. So, despite his regrets, Tom wound up studying harder than he ever had before.

After two weeks, the Grand Mage said the pupil was ready to try a simple transformation of a rock into a bowl. "Remember," the Grand Mage had intoned, "the twin keys to all magic, human or dragon, are focus and concentration.

The words of a spell are only the starting point for the enchantment. There are many factors to account for, such as breathing and even the pauses between syllables."

Running over the steps of the spell, Tom tried his best but the rock stubbornly stayed a rock. Instead, the Grand Mage's scales had changed to a shocking shade of pink.

"I'm sorry," the boy said, cringing as he waited for an angry tirade from such an important dragon.

However, the Grand Mage was too good a teacher to become upset by any pupil's mistakes and he had also warmed to Tom, even if he was a gasser. At first, the boy eyed the dragon uneasily as his scaled sides began to shake, and Tom heard a rumbling like lumps of coal being dumped into a bin. He was stunned when he realized the Grand Mage was chuckling. "Well, I don't think this color is very becoming, do you?"

"N-no," the startled boy stammered.

"As Longwhistle once said, wisdom is only gained through error." The Grand Mage easily changed himself back. "You are the first gas— I mean, human I have ever met, but you're not at all like the stories. I had my doubts at first about how much you could learn, but you have an aptitude for magic, Thomas."

Tom was surprised at the compliment. "But I keep making mistakes."

The Grand Mage folded his paws over his stomach and twiddled his claws thoughtfully. "But you are so amusing when you do that." He winked. "Here are two other important things to remember: Magic must always be respected, but that doesn't mean it can't be fun occasionally."

When Tom managed his first successful spell, he found he was beginning to enjoy magic and tried even harder, despite the dull parts and the continual embarrassment, for there were twenty failures for every success.

There were so many variables that Tom soon found that performing an enchantment correctly was a lot like trying to create a statue out of wet noodles. A week later when he had tried a simple spell to open scrolls, he accidentally endowed them with the power to giggle instead. Again the dragon chuckled, along with his library, in his rumbling, thumping fashion until he finally said, "Scrolls should be seen but not heard, don't you think, Master Thomas?" And he restored them to silence.

His cheeks reddening, Tom frowned at the now quiet scroll in front of him. "I would have sworn I did everything right. Maybe humans aren't meant to learn Dragon Lore."

The Grand Mage flicked a claw at Tom's hair. "Your tiger's blood may be changing you not only in body but in nature as well. Magic is much like music—indeed, many incantations must be sung rather than spoken. Just as each singer does his or her own version of a song, a wizard brings his or her own touch to the magic. Tigers are powerful creatures but they are wild, and so is their magic."

Tom squirmed uneasily, wondering just how far the transformation would go. "So that's why my spells are unpredictable?"

The Grand Mage tapped a claw on the scroll. "But that doesn't mean you should give up. Let's review the spell again."

Tom eventually got the hang of that enchantment, but he ran into trouble again when he tried to learn simple levitation. Instead of making a coral flagon rise from the table, he created dozens of tiny whirlpools that fluffed out the Grand Mage's plumes like a stretch of poodle hair. The dignified dragon twisted his long neck to consult the mirror on the wall—but it still reflected an empty room. He tapped the side. "This infernal thing is always running late." The image shimmered and became his own. "Well, in all my years of training mages, *this* never happened."

Tom slumped in his chair, wishing he knew how to become a snail and ooze away. "Sorry. I guess it came out as a wind spell."

The Grand Mage turned away and did not notice that the mirror mischievously insisted on keeping the ridiculous reflection. "My boy, I have seen many types of wind spells over the centuries, but none quite so refreshing as yours."

What Tom enjoyed learning even more than magic were the tales that lay behind them—which the ancient dragon also possessed in abundance.

When Tom asked the Grand Mage about the source of the dream stones, the old dragon hesitated. "It's a shameful episode that dragons do not like to mention," he admitted, and scratched a cheek, with a rasping sound like a file on steel. "But even if you're not kin by blood, you're kin by vocation and it would be a useful lesson: Be careful what you wish for—especially when it is the Empress granting it."

The Grand Mage might have been referring to a dragon empress, but Tom knew there was only one empress whose name people were reluctant to say. He touched the scale she had placed on his cheek and glanced at the dragon. When the Grand Mage nodded, Tom knew it had to be Nü Kua.

"Why do you have to be careful with wishes from her?" the boy asked.

"Because they are often as whimsical as they are dangerous," the Grand Mage explained. "After the victory over Kung Kung, the Empress had a dream in which Calambac and his family built her a magnificent palace, all of marble and gold, with a roof covered with giant pearls. There were many magical luxuries, and from the terraces she could view the wonders of the world. At a banquet with Calambac she mentioned this, and said the strange thing was that she returned to that palace every night in her dreams. As a joke, Calambac said he would present the bill later for the work that they had done in her dream, but his middle son—my ancestor Chukar—was greedy.

"'Since you love the palace we built for you in the dream and since you are able to delight in it each night,' Chukar promised, 'the price will be high.'

"Calambac laughed. 'Who can set a price upon a dream palace?'

"However, Chukar would not let the matter rest, even when his father finally rebuked him. 'You have gone beyond jesting. Leave it be.'

"'Father, you may do what you like,' Chukar persisted, 'but I wish to be paid for my labors in the Empress's dreams.'

"'Greed will be your undoing,' Calambac said. 'I will have none of this.'"

"And she blasted him right then and there?" Tom asked.

The Grand Mage spread out his paws. "No, the account says she was amused—but," he added, "she's far more dangerous when she seeks entertainment rather than vengeance. She told Chukar, 'A dream for a dream.'

"'I dream of a treasure,' Chukar said, and the Empress promised him payment equal to his desire.

"Chukar returned to his home, expecting a mountain of gold and jewels and pearls. He was surprised the next day to find a huge white stone the size of his palace."

"The first dream stone," Tom said.

"And the source for all the others," the Grand Mage said.

"What happened to Chukar?" the boy wondered.

The Grand Mage went on. "He was angry, of course. 'What is this worthless thing?' he said, and slapped it with a paw."

"And fell asleep," Tom said, remembering the effect on Mr. Hu.

"Not before he had curled himself so tight around the stone that no one could pry him from it," the Grand Mage said. "So Calambac in his wisdom used his magic to hide the stone and his son deep in an undersea canyon. Its location is revealed only to a few, who fetch bits of it for use. And there Chukar dreams of who knows what. Perhaps other treasures. Or perhaps that he is awake and performing all sorts of heroics."

"After all these centuries, I'm surprised there's anything left," Tom said.

"That's another of the Empress's jokes," the Grand Mage said. "No matter how much gets mined, the stone always replenishes itself. There are some who say that it's grown even larger over the centuries."

"So the dragons can dream as much as they like," Tom said. The more he heard of Nü Kua, the less he wanted to meet her again.

"Like Chukar. It's said that through the Empress's magic he still lives and lies next to the stone, dreaming of treasure." The Grand Mage swung his head so he could eye the boy sternly. "Well, once again you've managed to put off Elementary Thaumaturgy—but not anymore. Still, you've learned something about the nature of dreams."

"And dragons," Tom said.

The Grand Mage gave a cough. "I daresay," he said, and then unrolled the scroll. "Yes, well, the basis of the spell is this . . ." And the dragon went on in his dry voice.

As it turned out, Tom saw the Grand Mage more than his friends. He hardly ever saw Mistral or Sidney unless it was either of their turns to keep the Guardian company; for Mr. Hu was never left alone. On one of the rare occasions when he was together with the rat, Tom asked him what he was doing with all his time.

The rat only winked. "What do you think? I'm selling stuff. For every fancy noble in court, there's a hundred servants and soldiers. They're all eager for quality merchandise. I wish I'd found this place a long time ago. It's a gold mine—but even so, I'll be glad when Mr. H. wakes up for good. My customers have been telling me it's bad all over the kingdom. Some of them are even buying maps."

"What for?" Tom asked.

"They're thinking of emigrating to the upper realms," Sidney said with a grin. "When I get home, I'm going to set up a side business. You know, finding dragons places to live and work on land."

Tom scratched his head. "But everyone here thought it was a terrible punishment when Mistral was sent to land."

"Times have changed." Sidney shrugged.

The times had changed for the newly titled duchess as well. As part of the king's war council, she often came back subdued and silent. The one time the sympathetic boy had inquired if there was more bad news, Mistral had cut him off by saying it was confidential.

The one person who was consistently around was Monkey. When he was not with Mr. Hu, he was confined to his windowless room; and Monkey usually took the watch while Tom was at his lessons.

The only other company Tom saw were the dragon healers. Mr. Hu was quite a curiosity, and healers from all around the dragon kingdom flocked to see him. His room was often crowded whenever he was being examined. Tom received almost as thorough an inspection as they waited to see what effect the tiger's blood might have on him, for the sharing of life between two species was unprecedented and possible only with the Empress's powerful magic. To his growing uneasiness, he thought he saw light streaks in his hair the color of Mr. Hu's pelt.

One of the sights he never tired of was star rise in the evening and star fall in the morning. When she could leave the war council, Mistral would join him to watch the glowing lights.

In contrast to their time on land, his friend was reluctant now to discuss the dragons. When Tom asked her if she had heard from her branch of the clan, she told him that her brother sent back her letters, saying that he had no sister. "But that's no loss," she said. "He's such a bore. All he can talk about is hunting."

By now Tom understood the proud, lonely dragon enough to see through her mask of indifference. "Well, have you been able to talk to the jester then? He seemed to be a friend of yours," Tom asked, but Mistral replied that he was avoiding her.

"But then, what can I expect?" The dragon sighed. "My duchy was once his father's before it was confiscated."

She was more comfortable reminiscing about Mistress Lee, Tom's grandmother. Mistral had first met Mr. Hu when Mistress Lee had been taking care of her and Mr. Hu had been his grandmother's apprentice. Tom listened intently, for he had never heard these stories about his grandmother. These were the days before his father was born. He meant to ask Mr. Hu more about his father once the tiger was well, for Mr. Hu had also known him as a boy.

After Mr. Hu had abandoned the apprenticeship and returned to fight his own clan's wars, his path had crossed several times with Mistral's. Sometimes the dragon had been on his side and other times on the side of his enemy, the jackals.

"What happened to your sense of honor then?" Tom asked.

"I left it behind me in the dragon kingdom." Mistral gave the boy a crooked smile. "But don't worry. I've found it again. Blast these worms," she said, wriggling her shoulders.

"I shouldn't feel a thing through my armor, but I swear they make me itch." Plume worms had been planted on her scales as well as colored barnacles and other worms on her body, but for now they were little more than bumps that, with hundreds of pearls, formed the insignia of her duchy.

The tiger slept most of the time, purring often and even twitching occasionally, as if dreaming he were a young cub racing through the rain forest, so he seemed to be getting better. He woke only when the dragons took away the stone temporarily to serve him a meal. Tom always made a point of being there to feed the groggy Guardian, but the tiger had few words for his apprentice other than to ask if he was keeping up his studies in the Lore.

In addition to his schooling, Tom decided on his own that his apprenticeship would include acting as Mr. Hu's valet. Every day Tom made a point of cleaning the phoenix egg that sat on the table near the bed. He made it clear to all the servants that only he was to do that, and whenever he polished the egg with a piece of dragon silk, he thought he felt a brief warmth and a flash of light. Then he would brush Mr. Hu's suit and hat carefully.

Late one afternoon, his lessons ended early when the Grand Mage was summoned away to the war council. Tom returned to the rooms to relieve Monkey and, as he always did, went about his chores. As he finished with Mr. Hu's clothes, he felt the hard lump in the suit pocket and took out the green rock in which Räv and the hsieh were supposed to be trapped. Turning it around in his fingers, he found the dimple in the surface. He couldn't help wondering if that meant Mr. Hu's entrapment spell had failed and Räv had escaped after all. Had he seen her back at the museum? If it had really been Räv, why hadn't she attacked them earlier—perhaps when they had left the store and were at their most vulnerable?

And yet as dangerous as she was, Tom couldn't help feeling a little sorry for her. She'd been so mystified each time the boy had tried to save her. As tough and lonely a life as he had led, he could not conceive of a world where such decency was unexpected, but that seemed to be one in which she lived. Slipping the rock back into the pocket, he wished Räv dreams as sweet as Mr. Hu's—if she was indeed still inside the stone.

As he restored the clothes to the wardrobe, he wondered if he and his friends weren't trapped within their own version of the green rock, and if this wasn't all a dream. He could never get a straight answer from the healer on when Mr. Hu was going to be well enough to leave the kingdom. Her standard answer was always, "Be patient. The elderly do not always heal as fast."

Up to now, every day had brought more bad news for the dragons. What Mr. Hu had thought would be a safe refuge felt more and more like a trap waiting to spring shut. And Tom's apprenticeship, though he'd had some small successes with spells, did not seem to be going anywhere. His silly magic was more suitable for pranks than for defending himself against Vatten's monsters. He seemed no further along in his education than he had been before he entered the dragon kingdom.

Suddenly he felt as if the walls of the room were closing in on him, and his legs and feet had a restless life of their own, so he wound up walking back and forth, counting the steps to distract himself.

He had reached one thousand and seven when a tired Mistral entered. She smiled when she saw him pacing around the room. "You look like a tiger in a cage. In fact, you've got some of the stripes. All you need is a tail, and I'm sure the Grand Mage could arrange that," she teased.

Tom barely slowed. "Has the war council ended already?"

Mistral coiled up wearily beside the Guardian's bed and lowered her long neck so she could see both Mr. Hu and the rose. "1 . . . I left early. I have some things to think over."

Tom kept on pacing. "I'm surprised His Highness let you go."

The dragon rested her chin upon her paws, gazing up at the rose. "He was becoming rather upset with me so I thought it best if I left the room."

Tom glanced nervously at the tiger. What would they do if the king ordered them from the palace while Mr. Hu was still weak and helpless? "What did you do to annoy him?" the boy asked.

"His Highness . . . has need of certain services from me." The dragon kept her eyes upon the rose as she changed the subject. "Do you ever wonder at the irony in all this? The phoenix is a symbol of peace and yet it has caused so much fighting."

Before Tom could reply, he jumped back. "Ow!" he roared. A jellyfish lamp had stung him with its tentacles. They were such a constant problem that Monkey had even woven a net in his room to catch them. Tom leaped, sweeping his arm to create a current that sent the lamp tumbling away.

As the shadows cast by the rolling lamp flitted wildly around the room, Mistral said, "You're starting to remind me of Hu more and more. He would have struck at an enemy that way. All you need are claws. Have you considered growing your nails longer?"

Embarrassed, Tom hovered in the water. He really needed to get control of himself before the tiger blood took hold. "Don't even joke about it. What I really need to do is get out of here." He caught himself, remembering that this was Mistral's home. "I mean, it's not so bad for a vacation."

Mistral gently blew another jellyfish lamp away from the boy. "I grow tired of these endless councils, and I have no time for anything else. His Highness can be rather persistent with his views. I'm beginning to think exile was better than a title."

His friend looked so exhausted and upset that Tom felt sorry for her. "Maybe you should go back to the land."

"Not until Hu can go home." Mistral sat up on her hind legs. "I can put up with anything as long as I must."

Tom drew the curtains aside but it was still too early for star rise. However, the Fire Gardens caught his eye. Maybe that would distract both of them. "It'd be good to get out of the palace. What about a swim around the grounds? I'll ask Monkey to watch Mr. Hu."

Though she still looked tired, Mistral nodded. "Yes, that might be just the thing."

Yet when they entered the Fire Gardens, Mistral swam listlessly, as if her mind were on other things.

"Can't you tell me a little about what the king wants from you?" Tom asked his friend.

Mistral patted him on the shoulder. "All I can tell you is that His Highness knows he wants a great favor, but to be fair to him, he has a great need."

"Not for a fool," a voice said, "for nowadays there's enough foolishness here for all." Rising from where he had been hiding in the gardens was Uncle Tumer.

"Ring Neck," Mistral said in surprise.

"I am unworthy of that name. Uncle Tumer is what fits me now," the Fool corrected her.

Mistral chuckled. It sounded like water rippling over pebbles, and Tom could not recall hearing her sound so relaxed before this. "The Duchess of the Flaming Hills may call you what she likes. But you've avoided me until now," Mistral said, touching the Fool's living cap and making the leechlike fish writhe in response. "Why seek me out today?"

Uncle Tumer hunched his shoulders. "It's taken this long to work up my courage. It would have been foolish."

"Well, aren't you a fool?" Mistral demanded.

"But a cowardly fool," Uncle Tumer said.

"You say some pretty insulting things to the king," Tom said.

Uncle Tumer's bells jingled when he shrugged. "I know how far I dare go."

Mistral cleared her throat in embarrassment. "I thought you were avoiding me because you resented my receiving the duchy that once belonged to your father."

Uncle Tumer lifted his head. "The duchy is no gift anymore. His Highness is not the king of dragons but the prince of fools if he thinks he has kept the news secret. There is little he can keep from me. To everyone I'm just his footstool—but I've heard how Vatten's monsters have smashed everything at the duchy. When my father was alive, he kept the Clan of the Nine away, but I wonder if even he could have protected us nowadays."

Tom felt himself growing angry at the king for tricking Mistral that way. How could the king have given her a ruined duchy and called it a great gift? But when the boy started to growl deep in his throat, he checked himself.

Mistral floated in the water for a moment. Then she roused herself with a wriggle of her shoulders. "If it is my fate to have to fight for everything I want, so be it! I will go to my duchy and hoist my banner to let all our enemies know that it is *my* land now."

The jester's eyes shined with admiration. "My father would have said you deserved it for being the only one to defend him. There were so many to praise him when he was the Shield of the Dragons. And yet behind his back the jealous nobles were filling His Highness's ears with lies that he was planning to usurp the throne. And no one spoke up when His Highness ordered my father's imprisonment."

Mistral's face softened as she regarded Uncle Tumer. "What turned my old friend into a clown?"

"Cowardice and then madness and then cowardice again," Uncle Tumer admitted. "When you said what I should have said and then were sent into exile, I can't tell you how ashamed I was."

"I warned you to go with me," Mistral said.

Uncle Tumer sounded sad. "I couldn't leave while my father was in prison, and when my father died there, the grief overwhelmed me. I should have followed you to the upper realms."

There was a long pause before Mistral said, "I would have welcomed the company."

"I told you I was a coward," Uncle Tumer said as he drifted along. "To live in the upper realms where the sun sucks the very life from you was too harsh for me. Any life in the sea, even one of humiliation, was preferable."

"But you were endangering yourself by staying," Tom said.

"I knew eyes would be watching me and so I pretended to lose my wits," the Fool said. "And for a long time, between the guilt and sorrow, I might not have been pretending anymore. I came here and claimed the role of fool for myself. I knew that His Highness would suspect nothing if I played the fool right before his eyes, and it suited his whim. When folk see me, they think of how merciful he is."

"I think you have had as bad a time as I," Mistral said gently.

"No," Uncle Tumer said, "I've lived in luxury—even if I was risking the loss of my head at any moment. But I wanted to tell you that I admire what you are doing for the Guardian."

"That's enough." Mistral cut him off, glancing at the boy self-consciously. "I'm not doing anything very worthy of admiration."

Suddenly trumpets blew shrilly. "Alarm! Alarm!" a dragon guard bellowed.

CHAPTER SEVEN

T he whole sea mount began to vibrate with the sound of the great gongs. They saw the guards overhead swirl into tight cone formations. Mistral pulled Tom out of the way of more guards pouring from the main gate. As they watched them race past to form up, she looked stunned. "But the Winter Palace is deep within the kingdom. How could anyone attack here?"

The fish of Uncle Tumer's cap continued to wriggle even after he had finished nodding his head. "If your duchy can lie in ruins, nothing is safe from attack anymore."

"A scarred land suits a scarred duchess. All my dreams turn out this way," Mistral said bitterly.

"Is it Vatten coming for the egg?" Tom asked, looking all around at the surrounding ocean. It was hard to believe that the sunlit waters could hide any monsters.

"If the Nameless One is Vatten's creature," Mistral said

smugly, "he'll learn his mistake soon."

The sea churned as armored dragons swarmed out of the palace like angry bees out of a hive, but every dragon seemed to know his or her place, assembling quickly into more cone formations. Sunlight glittered from their steel scales like deadly raindrops, and banner fishes with large fins and brightly decorated sides hovered at the point of each unit. Soon the surface of the sea was hidden by what seemed like a sheaf of deadly arrows poised and waiting to be loosed.

Mistral swelled with pride. "You are about to see what few humans have, Master Thomas. The Imperial Guard is going to war."

The king himself swam from his palace with the Grand Mage and a dozen other courtiers of varying lengths. Lifting a paw for silence, the king announced, "The enemy has dared to come here, a place sacred in dragon memory. You are the bravest of the brave. Defend our honor. Defend our pride."

Hundreds of dragons clashed steel-tipped claws in answer so that the sea rang with the sound, and hundreds of voices shouted, "We will!"

"Isn't that the finest sight?" Mistral murmured to Tom. Like the warrior she was, her chest swelled with pride and her tail was twitching with eagerness.

Conch shells blew the advance and the dragon formations, plumes flying, launched themselves toward the west as if shot from dozens of bows. Their swift passage raised a current that rippled across the garden and sent Tom against his friend.

Despite his bold words, the king anxiously watched as the guard disappeared into the distance.

As Mistral lifted the boy away from her, she said, "I see you spoke the truth, Your Highness, when you said no place was safe. Not even here."

The king swung his head around. "I have not lied to you, nor have I exaggerated. We have great need of your services. Will you do as I asked of you?"

Mistral's shoulders slumped. "You ask so much."

"I would not ask it if our kind were not suffering everywhere," the king replied. "But you must do what your heart tells you. Come inside now. We are shutting all the gates."

The king spun his large body around as nimbly as an eel and disappeared inside, followed closely by his court.

Mistral started after him but then stopped, twisting her head to the west where the guard had gone. "It is hard to stand idle when our kin may soon be dying."

The jester glanced nervously at the gates that were closing with loud groans. "We should do what His Highness commands."

Mistral stared at him in disappointment. "You'd play the coward even now?"

"The Royal Fool is one thing, the Nameless One

another." Uncle Tumer hesitated, then lowered his head. Even his living cap drooped. "I can only be what I am."

Mistral listened to the conch shells fading in the distance. "I can't hide in safety while others die defending me."

Poor Mistral, Tom thought. After so many years of combat on the land, she had returned home to live in peace—only to find more fighting. "You're a duchess now," he argued. "It's not your job to fight."

Uncle Tumer swam in front to block her. "The gasser boy is right," he pleaded.

Mistral stared at him contemptuously. "I'll take no advice from a fool and a coward like you." Raising a foreleg, she knocked the jester to the side with a loud jangling of his bells and then sprang up in the water, plunging toward the battle.

With a lump in his throat, Tom watched her leap upward and dart away. "Was she always like that?"

"Always," Uncle Tumer said, trying to calm the bell fish. "But there was a time when I would have gone with her."

Tom looked at the forlorn dragon. "I don't know if I would have stood up to the whole dragon kingdom either."

"Mistral did." Uncle Tumer floated in a sad circle as if wanting to follow her but unable.

Tom heard a loud thud and turned to see that the main gate had closed. From around the sea mount, he heard more thumps as side gates were also closed.

"We must go inside," the jester said, "or we'll be shut out."

The Grand Mage had lingered and he raised a paw. "Come, Thomas. A gas— I mean a human has no place out here."

Even though Tom knew there was little he could do to help the dragons, he felt it would be wrong to hide in safety when his friend was risking her life. He desperately tried to think of some magic that would help them. "I wish you had taught me some combat spells."

"It would only have made you reckless at times such as these," the Grand Mage said with an affectionate shake of his head. He wriggled his claws. "Now come."

Uncle Tumer coiled frantically as the gates continued to close. "We must go."

Tom gave a kick in the opposite direction. "You do what you want."

"I . . . I will." Uncle Tumer gulped and with an apologetic dip of his head he fled. Soon the jester was only a speck and his jingling bells a faint memory.

"I command you to come inside," the Grand Mage insisted, beckoning to him sternly. "I know a side gate we can use."

Tom wanted to flee with Uncle Tumer, but he also knew that neither his grandmother nor Mr. Hu would have deserted a friend. He hadn't wanted the apprenticeship at first and the actual Guardianship even less, but having accepted them, he at least had to try to be worthy of them. Mr. Hu and his friends seemed to think Tom was up to the task.

So instead of escaping, Tom gave a kick of his legs and began to swim away. "I'm sorry," he said, putting more distance between himself and the elderly dragon, "but I'm not *your* apprentice."

The Grand Mage drew in water sharply so that his nostrils quivered. "But what can you do, *apprentice*? You have neither claws nor powerful enough magic yet."

"But you do," the boy challenged.

"Another basic rule of magic is to know your limits," the Grand Mage snapped. "And I know mine."

"Well, I haven't learned mine," the boy shot back.

As Tom kept churning through the water, the dragon stood torn, as if he would follow, but finally he turned and reluctantly disappeared as well.

When the final set of gates closed, the palace fell silent. Tom began to feel very alone and small as he glided over the gardens. Even the animals had closed up into tight knobs and little tufts like the knots of an unfinished tapestry. He had begun to regret his words to the Grand Mage. The dragon was right. What could he really do in a fight? Against the Nameless One his magic would be as puny as his fists.

Suddenly the sea began to ripple, tugging him first in one direction and then another; in the distance he saw several glittering dots that swiftly grew larger as they swam toward him until he could see they were dragons. He thought they were messengers with news of the battle, but then he saw their terrified faces as they jetted past him.

More of the Imperial Guard poured after them in retreat, all order gone. In a panic, they kicked and wriggled, each intent on saving his or her own life. In their midst, he thought he saw Tench, frantically shoving other dragons out of his way. As Tom tumbled about in the wake of their passage, he heard them cry, "The Nameless One, the Nameless One!"

"We're doomed," shouted another.

When Tom finally righted himself, the survivors had already vanished into the vastness of the ocean. The next moment he heard wild wailing that made him look around, wondering if a funeral procession was coming. And then he saw what seemed like a giant scarf gliding toward him.

It kept growing larger and larger until Tom saw it must be at least a hundred feet in length and perhaps twenty feet in diameter. Long ropes trailed down, so that it looked more like the white fringe that had been ripped from the bottom of a giant curtain. From the way the sand stuck to the tips, he assumed there was some sticky coating on them.

When he saw the ribbons and organs pulsing within the translucent sides, he realized it was alive. And tattooed over and over upon the translucent flesh he saw the number nine with a curled serpentine tail—the symbol of Vatten's followers. This was truly a living nightmare that Vatten had sent to plague the dragons.

Dozens of giant bean-shaped balloons ran along its sides, also tattooed. The wails were issuing from the many bell-shaped mouths, each about the size of Tom, that covered the strange being.

Tom's eyes were drawn to a dark shape wriggling within one balloon, wondering what organ that might be. To his horror, he suddenly realized it must be a dragon. The balloons were stomachs and the dangling ropes were tentacles. The mouths didn't look big enough to swallow a dragon, but they must stretch somehow. This huge monstrosity could only be the Nameless One.

Not all the guard had fled. A dozen dragons still swam around it, trying to halt it, when one of the tentacles shot forward. With a shrill cry, the fleeing dragon squirmed, trying to break free but unable to as the tentacle lifted it toward a mouth that was already eagerly stretching wide.

More dragons were drawn up into the mouths as if they were no more than flies. Victims were being deposited in the bellies running along the creature where the walls constricted, holding them trapped until they were digested. Suddenly he recognized the dragon still struggling within a belly. It was Mistral.

The sight of his imprisoned friend sent a wave of anger flooding through him, washing away his doubts and fears and thoughts of escape. He was a Guardian after all—even if it was only temporary—and he had to try to be as brave and noble as his predecessors and rescue his friend.

He felt as if his grandmother and all the Guardians before her were gathering alongside him to do battle. With all their wisdom and power, they would have thrown back their sleeves and cast lightning bolts, but what magic could Tom do? Suddenly he remembered the whirlpools he had made in the Grand Mage's study. If he could create one large enough, perhaps he could distract the monster long enough to save his friend somehow.

It was easier to make a mistake than to repeat it, however, and he growled in frustration. Yet the ghostly presence of the past Guardians encouraged him so that he kept on muttering spells as the creature drew closer and closer.

It was the eighth try that did it. He felt a tug on his sleeve as the water began to whirl and he waited for a vortex. It never came. Instead, he felt a tug on his other sleeve, then another and another.

He tried to see his friend but the water had begun to blur, obscuring the monster. He'd done it!

He looked eagerly for the spectacle of a giant whirlpool, but what he saw was one, two, three . . . thousands of tiny whirlpools hiding the monster from sight. In his bungling effort he had managed to create not one giant but a herd of miniatures. He'd failed as an apprentice yet again.

While the whirlpools had no impact on its thick body when the Nameless One tried to pass through, its tentacles began to twitch and jerk as they automatically sought to catch the spinning columns of water. Confused, the monster halted abruptly, its mouths bellowing in deeper, frightened notes, its tentacles now out of control as they flailed about in a vain hunt for the little whirlpools.

With a kick of his legs, Tom swam toward where he thought Mistral was. The Nameless One grew before him like a huge ghostly wall; the tiny whirlpools pulled and prodded like dozens of hands and it was hard to see.

Squinting as he turned in the churning water, Tom headed directly into a spot where a current had swept dozens of little whirlpools together like a flock of startled birds. The boy was knocked from side to side and round and round, helpless in the spell of his own making.

He tried to break free but could not stop the spiraling and tumbling until suddenly something caught his ankles. With a cry, he fought against what he thought was a tentacle but then he heard Mistral say, "What are you doing here?"

He looked over his shoulder to see the dragon, her armorlike hide proof against the whirlpools. He was dangling upside down from her paw like a fisherman's catch.

"I came to rescue you," Tom explained sheepishly, "but it seems to be the other way around."

Mistral held up the sharp claws of her free paw. "It just

took me a while to cut through. It's thick like rubber." She shook a tiny whirlpool away from her eyes. "Is this your doing?"

"Yes," Tom said, "but it's not what I wanted. I'm sorry. I'm an awful apprentice."

With a kick of her powerful legs, Mistral plunged them away from the monster and the whirlpools. "Sometimes it's more important to have luck than skill," she said. "The creature has no eyes but it can feel. It hunts mainly by touch, and the whirlpools are confusing it. Well done."

It was only the second time his magic had been praised. The boy smiled. Maybe he was starting to get the hang of being a Guardian.

Behind them, the Nameless One was coiling and twisting, trying to shake off its watery tormentors, but the whirlpools clung to it as if glued.

"How do we stop it?" Tom asked, trying to catch his breath.

"It doesn't have a head," Mistral said, "and no central nervous system that I can tell. I think it's a giant colonial animal that's made up of many individual cells, so you can't kill it. When we managed to cut off one section, both pieces kept right on fighting. While I was battling one part, the other got me. All we managed to do was create two Nameless Ones."

"Your Grace!" a dragon cried happily. "You're safe." A few brave members of the Imperial Guard surrounded her.

"We came as soon as we could get away."

In the distance, Tom could see the other section of the monster Mistral had mentioned, floating toward them with equal malevolence.

"I'm here thanks to the Guardian's apprentice," Mistral said with a nod to Tom. "Mr. Hu made the right choice when he picked him."

Despite the menace of the Nameless One, Tom felt elated. He'd lived up to the Guardianship.

"How do we destroy this thing?" another guard asked in frustration.

Mistral gazed beyond the palace toward the fiery red dots that marked the mouths of the other volcanoes along the ridge line. "I have an idea, but first we rescue the others."

It was a dangerous game the dragons played, for the monster's tentacles flailed unpredictably and the mouths reached for anything that came near, but sharp claws managed to free the dragons' trapped comrades and they led them back to Tom.

"Can you lift the spell?" Mistral asked the boy.

"That much I do remember," Tom said. The Grand Mage had driven that lesson into his head as the first thing any beginner should learn.

"The rest of you withdraw to a safe distance," Mistral ordered.

"We can't leave you, Your Grace," one of the guards protested.

"It's my wish," Mistral said. "This is my responsibility alone."

"But—" one of them began.

"Alone," Mistral insisted.

The guard bowed his head. "As you command."

By the time they retreated to a safe distance the other, smaller section of the creature had drawn dangerously close. The dragon guards had done a great deal of damage to it. Half its tentacles were missing and many of its bellies sagged like deflated balloons and several of its mouths were in tatters, but it still looked hungry and ready for a fight.

"Once you stop the spell, leave me," Mistral said to Tom.

"I can't do that," Tom said.

Mistral glanced at the boy and then back at the advancing piece of the monster. "I thank you for being a loyal friend, but you owe this to Mr. Hu. He put you in charge of the phoenix."

Tom knew the dragon was right, but the Guardianship had never felt heavier. "What can you do against them?"

She smiled grimly. "Don't worry. I plan to live a long time—if only to annoy that stupid ape."

Reassured, the boy agreed. "All right."

Mistral lowered her head. "*Now.*"

It only took a moment to end the spell, then Tom watched as his friend shot like an arrow toward the main monster, her legs drawn in tight against her sides so she could move even faster. Tentacles rose, but she dodged them as nimbly as a mosquito, and then, flying along the main trunk of the Nameless One, she lowered all her paws, raking its side with her claws.

As she passed over each mouth, it began to scream angrily and the tentacles whipped this way and that, trying to seize its tormentor, but Mistral was too fast, slicing a good deal of the monster before she turned to the second section of the creature and tormented it the same way.

Tom watched breathlessly as Mistral hovered, raising her head. "Who are you to come to the palace without His Highness's permission?"

The two sections of the monster sounded like a whistle factory gone berserk as they wheeled around, trying to grab her.

With a laugh, Mistral swam over the gardens, taunting and teasing the two pieces, which followed her away from the palace toward the volcanoes.

Tom did his best to keep sight of his friend, but Mistral was soon hardly more than a speck and Tom could no longer hear her, yet he knew she was leading the monsters on with her voice. Then he could see the monster pieces had turned pink in the lurid glare from a volcano top.

Suddenly Mistral dove into the volcano.

"No!" Tom yelled uselessly.

Both monstrous sections dropped like lead weights,

tentacles reaching for her until the tips touched the surface of the lava and twitched back. Too late, the pieces tried to pull up. Shrieking in fright, they both fell into the volcano.

Tom ached for his friend—or it was more like an emptiness that kept widening within him. Once a water main had broken underneath a street, washing away the supporting dirt so that the asphalt top had collapsed. He had watched as the street crumbled, the edges widening faster and faster violently. Except now the crumbling was in his heart.

Yet it felt strangely familiar—not like when his grandmother had died, because there had been so much happening. But when? And then it was as if a door had been unlocked and the memories came flooding into his mind, and he remembered the moment his grandmother had told him his parents were lost and probably dead. The sense of emptiness had frightened him so much that he had shut it out.

"She was a great lady," a guardswoman said sadly.

Suddenly Tom did a somersault in the water and pointed at the speck coming toward them. "She still is," he roared. He waved to Mistral, and the dragon waved back.

CHAPTER EIGHT

E ven though patches of her scales were burned from the volcano's fires and her plumes and decorations were singed, in Tom's mind there wasn't another gilded and jeweled courtier who could match Mistral.

"Well," the boy said with a tired smile, "we've survived another battle."

"But can we survive the next one?" Mistral asked somberly as the guards who had fought with her gathered around her.

"Are you hurt?" Tom asked.

Mistral craned her long neck around. "I've just lost some insignia, and that's no loss. There's plenty more at court."

From behind them, they heard the great gates groan open again. The dragons within the palace had watched Mistral's victory, and now that it was safe they began to flood toward her. The jester led them all. "Let me take you to the healer right away."

Mistral gave Uncle Tumer a glare that would have wilted any creature but a dragon and made the palace dragons halt in midwater. "So you've decided to come out now that it's safe."

"I told you I was no hero," Uncle Tumer mumbled.

Mistral pointedly presented her back to him. "Get out of my sight, coward."

Tom felt sorry for the Fool as he slunk away. "He was scared."

Mistral swung her head around. "And weren't you when you came to rescue me? But that didn't stop you."

"I didn't do a very good job of it." He smiled. "You wound up saving me."

Mistral waved a kindly paw. "You did plenty and you'll get better with practice, my boy."

"If the practice doesn't kill me first," Tom said.

A battered guardswoman raised a paw. "Three cheers for Her Grace! She's saved us!"

Tired as she was, Mistral was so angry that she spiraled up through the water like a whirlpool and then hung suspended. "Fools! I've saved no one." She flung a paw toward the volcano. "The Nameless One may be gone, but the Clan of the Nine remains. And how can we replace all the bold warriors who have already been destroyed?"

The crowd fell silent, staring up at the angry duchess

who hovered over them like a black dagger.

"Your Grace," the Grand Mage reproved her from somewhere within the crowd. "This is neither the time nor the place to speak of such things."

Mistral's chest rose and fell. "It's time to stop hiding the truth. We dragons have been terribly weakened and the kingdom is in peril!"

The Grand Mage swam through the intimidated throng. "I think that's something you should take up with His Highness. Shall we go?" he asked pointedly.

Mistral turned to her battle mates. "Would you clear a way for my friend and me?"

"At once, Your Grace," the guardswoman said, and she and her fellow guard forced the courtiers back, creating a kind of tunnel within the dense pack so that Mistral and Tom could swim through.

Uncle Tumer humbly followed them; his ribbons shaking and bells jingling urgently. "The Royal Fool must have his lowly fool."

As they swam into the throng, the Grand Mage joined them. "You must forgive us, Your Grace, if we want to celebrate a triumph. We have had such dire news of late."

"I suppose we have to keep our spirits up," Mistral conceded grudgingly.

Courtiers and servants eagerly crowded in from all directions, and it was all that their escort of battered warriors could do to keep a passage open. As they swam into the palace, congratulations rained down upon them.

When they came to the courtroom, the Grand Mage said to Tom, "We must part here, but that was bravely done. I'm glad you proved me wrong."

The boy couldn't lie to the kindly dragon. "I messed up the spell," he admitted to his teacher.

The Grand Mage leaned forward to whisper so only Tom could hear. "I will tell you the real secret to magic: Make people think your mistakes are not mistakes at all but part of your plan from the very beginning. There's many an apprentice who has begun worse—including myself."

Feeling encouraged, Tom returned to their rooms where the disguised sentry smiled at him for the first time. "Good for you, gasser. I wish I could have had a go at that monster. I've lost a lot of good friends to it."

Inside Mr. Hu's bedroom, Sidney shouted, "Hooray!" He tried to throw confetti he had stored somewhere in his fur but the paper simply hung in soggy bits.

Monkey somersaulted through the water. "Well done, Tom! We watched from the windows but we couldn't see everything, so tell us all the details."

Perhaps I'm not such a terrible apprentice after all, Tom thought.

"How's Mr. Hu?" Tom asked, looking anxiously at his master. The tiger lay on his bed sleeping while the rose lay upon its table.

"Don't worry about him. He slept through it peaceful

as a cub." Monkey heaped some cushions on a bench. "Now sit. I want to hear all about the battle."

Sidney set down a bowl of candied slugs. "Have some? These things aren't bad once you get used to them. Some of them aren't dead yet so they kind of wiggle a little as they go down. Monkey's being squeamish."

Tom had thought nothing could put off the ape. He told his friends about the battle. Sidney began to pop slugs into his mouth by the pawful as he grew more excited.

When Tom was finished, Monkey said with a fondness he would never have shown directly, "I bet that lizard's head is twice as big now."

"I don't think so," Tom said. "She seems to think the dragons are still in trouble even though the Nameless One is dead." He told them what Mistral had said.

The empty bowl upon his lap, Sidney licked his claws. "So I say we get Mr. H. back on his hind paws and out of here as soon as we can."

For once, Monkey looked somber. "Yes, the sooner the better."

When the healer arrived for her daily visit to her patient, they asked her when she thought Mr. Hu would be healthy enough to leave, but she would give them no prediction. "These things take time," she said, refusing to look at them as she fussed over the tiger. "And I've said the elderly heal at their own pace."

When Mistral returned to their rooms that evening, she glanced nervously first at Mr. Hu and then at the rose. The rat took the opportunity to rush up and throw some new confetti he had made by industriously tearing kelp leaves into bits. "Hooray!"

Mistral waved her paw back and forth, scattering the kelp about the room. "There's nothing to cheer about, you silly rat." Their friend seemed more nervous and irritable than ever. Only new disasters in other parts of the kingdom could have spoiled her tremendous victory.

"Maybe the star rise will take your mind off things," Tom said helpfully, starting to draw the curtains.

"Bah, leave them closed," Mistral said with another wave of her paw. "I'm not in the mood tonight."

Monkey cleared his throat. "You must be tired after your splendid fight. Why don't you have a rest? I don't mind taking a double shift."

Mistral lunged forward so that her snout was right against the ape's muzzle. "I keep my word, unlike some furbags."

Monkey gently pushed her snout away. "I was just trying to—"

"I don't need help from thieves," Mistral snapped.

Monkey picked up his staff. "Try to do a dragon a favor and that's the thanks I get." And he stomped out to be escorted back to his own room.

Sidney sidled over to the dragon as she coiled herself

113

up in a menacing heap. "You know what always cheers me up?" he suggested. "I buy something." He started to reach into his fur. "Now I give a real nice discount to a hero."

Mistral raised a paw with daggerlike claws. "And I don't need your idiotic chatter either."

Sidney could be the most persistent salesperson in the world, but the menace in the dragon's voice and eyes was unmistakable. "Well," the rat said with a nervous grin, "if you change your mind, I'll be around."

When the rat had scurried away as well, Tom clasped his hands behind his back. "I guess you must have heard something bad from the king, but that's no reason to take it out on your friends."

"I don't need anyone," Mistral said, laying her chin upon her curled body. "I've always managed on my own."

Tom rubbed his head. "I used to think that too. But now I have Mr. Hu and Sidney and Monkey and you. And it's a lot better that way."

Mistral scratched deep gouges into the floor with her hind claws. "You'll soon find out that fool ape is more trouble than he's worth. And as for the rest of you, you'll be gone soon enough."

"We're your friends," Tom insisted. "We'll stay as long as we can help."

"I was talking about how long you'll live." Mistral slapped a paw against the floor in frustration. "Dragons live for centuries and centuries. You'll flit around and then die in what a dragon would consider the blink of an eye."

It took a moment for Tom to overcome his shock at her insensitive remark. He wondered if he had sounded as angry and miserable before he'd met Mr. Hu. "I know you're worried, but you really shouldn't be rude."

"Don't lecture me on manners." Mistral rested her chin back upon her coils. "Dragons were building palaces when the ancestors of humans were still in trees."

"A pedigree isn't a license to be mean," Tom argued.

Mistral's eyes narrowed. "What would a mongrel like you know about pedigrees? You're not even human anymore. You're half tiger now."

Before Tom could deny it, the Grand Mage knocked upon the open door. His gaze rested on the rose and then he shuffled inside. "Ah, there you are," the elderly dragon said. "Time to finish your lessons. We really can't have you falling behind in your studies even for a day, can we?"

For once, Tom was glad he had to study. "No, we can't."

The Grand Mage bowed to Mistral. "Your Grace, have you considered His Highness's proposal?"

Mistral looked away but she nodded reluctantly. "Yes," she said softly. "Tell him I will do as he asked."

"Capital!" The Grand Mage beamed and gave Tom a gentle shove. "Then let's be off."

Tom whirled around in the doorway to tell Mistral that her title had gone to her head. But when he saw her staring dejectedly at the rose, he swallowed his words.

He found that the enterprising rat had traveled no farther than the hallway, where Sidney had set out some items for the sentry to select. "I'll bring the can of car polish to you later," Sidney promised the Grand Mage as the rat exited the room.

"You have a car?" Tom asked the Grand Mage, puzzled.

The Grand Mage stroked his chin whiskers in embarrassment. "No, but I find it does wonders for bringing out the luster of my scales."

Despite everything, Tom had to smile. Leave it to the resourceful rat to find a way to prosper even at the bottom of the ocean.

When Tom returned late that evening and entered Mr. Hu's bedroom, he began to feel uneasy, as if ants were crawling up and down his spine. "Something . . . is wrong," he said, looking about the room.

For once, both Sidney and Monkey were there at the same time and happened to be playing dominoes together, using specially trained snails with markings on their shells. Sidney paused with a domino in his paw, its footpad wriggling, and surveyed his surroundings. "It seems the same to me. What feels funny to you?"

Monkey waited patiently for Sidney to make his play. "You mean something besides how long it's taking Hu to heal? There's Mistral's temper, but for all their armored hides, dragons are the most sensitive creatures inside.

Who knows what upset her?"

Tom tried to understand it himself. "I guess those are both part of it, but there's more." The itchiness was so bad that he was wriggling, wanting to scratch.

The ape saw him fidgeting. "Maybe humans can get that unmentionable problem that dragons have."

Sidney was more direct. "If you want, I can trade for some scale lice powder for you."

Tom scratched his arm but the itchiness only spread through his body. "I can't help scratching." He began to pace back and forth restlessly. "It's like there's something bubbling inside."

"Your tiger blood's stirring in you." Monkey peered at him closely. "Oh yes, I'd say there's flecks of yellow in your eyes."

"There are?" Tom checked his reflection in a mirror, but everything seemed normal.

Monkey plopped down on a chaise lounge with a loud laugh. "I was just joking. You were taking things too seriously. You're as easy to tease as Hu."

"Ha, ha, very funny," Tom muttered as he turned to where Mr. Hu still slept. As he watched the tiger's chest rise and fall in slow, even breaths beneath the silk covers, the Guardian's last instructions came back to his apprentice: Trust your nose rather than your eyes because nothing is as it appears.

He looked around the room, but everything seemed right. Still, he couldn't shake the uneasy feeling. He began prowling about the room, testing the water with his nose as Mr. Hu had instructed.

Everything appeared normal until he came to the rose. There was something lifeless about it, but he could not say what until he finally smelled it. "Does the rose have a funny scent to you?" he asked, smelling it from several directions as he circled around.

Monkey sniffed several times and then shook his head. "No, does it to you?"

"The petals have a faint whiff of dragon." Crouching over the rose intently, as if it were his prey, Tom examined it more closely. There was no tiny spark of life inside, only a solid dullness.

Monkey peered at the rose until his face was almost touching it. Then he straightened with a clap of his paws. "I don't notice anything different."

"Me neither," Sidney said after a quick test with his nostrils.

Tom rubbed the back of his neck. "It doesn't feel right. And it doesn't smell right either."

Monkey tilted his head to the side as he gazed at the boy thoughtfully. "But then my nose was never as sensitive as Hu's. And you do have some of his blood in you now."

The more Tom gazed at the rose, the more certain he was that it was a forgery. If only Mr. Hu were awake, he would know, but he wasn't. Instead, the tiger had trusted the egg to Tom. "I don't think this is the phoenix egg," he finally said. "It's all wrong. I think the dragons may have taken the real one and replaced it with this fake."

"The dragons may have been in a hurry when they created the imitation. They got the look and feel right, but they might have gotten a little careless with the smell." Monkey rubbed his muzzle. "Though their snouts may be longer than a tiger's, they're not as good. So you're absolutely sure?"

Though his instincts said it was a forgery, Tom had to admit, "Not completely."

Sidney raised a paw for attention. "Excuse me, but what can we do if this really is a fake? We're in the middle of an ocean surrounded by dragons."

"We have Mistral," Tom said.

Sidney looked sad. "Or is she part of the con? We'd better play our cards close to the vest until we know for sure."

"First, let's see if the real phoenix egg is somewhere else," the practical ape suggested. "If the dragons have stolen it, we'll work out something."

Tom nodded toward the hallway beyond the door where the disguised sentry was waiting. "But you're stuck either here or in your room."

"Not all of me," Monkey said, and tugged his cap into a rakish angle. "Why do you think I went before the entire dragon court with a bald tail?"

Suddenly Tom understood. "So you could promise the

king that what he saw would stay in the room, but that didn't apply to the little apes."

Monkey chuckled. "You also have to learn a few things about tricking dragons." Then from his tail he plucked a handful of hairs and blew on them. "Change," he said.

Instantly dozens of little sea horses with yellow bodies and long purple fins wriggled around him like gnats. "Go, children, and tell me what you see and hear. Some of you follow Mistral and some of you trail the Grand Mage."

"And smell," Tom said, remembering Mr. Hu's advice. He couldn't see what harm it would do to nose around. "And I will too."

"I'll check things on my rounds," Sidney promised.

When he finished his lessons the next day with the newly shined Grand Mage, Tom surprised his teacher by requesting a trip to see Calambac's moss collection.

It was housed in the lower levels of the palace, which were even vaster than he had first thought. But everywhere he found decay as the dragons concentrated on the war rather than upon repairs. There were whole suites of rooms where barnacles and other creatures had covered the furniture.

The collection itself proved as boring as the boy had suspected it would be. However, the wizard treated each piece of moss as if it were a treasure, for he was a true scholar in whose eyes moss and gems had equal value. He never noticed the half-dozen little sea horses watching his every move.

When they left the chamber where the collection was housed, they swam back to the channel that connected all the levels in the palace. "Read the next chapter in *Alchemical Metamorphoses* by tomorrow, Master Thomas," the Grand Mage said, and gave Tom a gentle shove toward the higher levels.

While Tom paddled slowly upward, he saw the Grand Mage descend, his tail flicking urgently as he picked up speed. With a flip, Tom began to follow the wizard at a distance.

The lower they went, the darker it seemed to become, and it became hard to keep the Grand Mage in sight. He did not think the palace could go any deeper, and yet the Grand Mage continued on. When the dragon finally ducked into a doorway of one level, Tom trailed him.

If anything, the neglect was even worse on that floor, where worms and barnacles had grown over everything. There were nooks and crannies in hallways that had once been smooth, and some of the corridors had narrowed so that even the smallest dragon could not have squeezed through.

The Grand Mage knew his way through the warren, but the boy did not. To his dismay, he finally lost the wizard and so he began to search on his own, making marks on the corridor walls so he could retrace his steps.

He gave a start when he heard the laughter of a dragon child from a hallway, but the entrance narrowed to a hole that would not have admitted his fist. It was possible some young dragon had shrunk itself to enter, but Tom thought of what the gossipy servant had said about ghosts. Who knew what stories were true about the ancient palace?

The rooms had all been deserted, so he was surprised when he found an area that was alive with activity. He peeked into a huge chamber where dragons with glowing healing designs bustled about under the soft light cast by pastel jellyfish.

More dragons of all ages and sizes lay sleeping on ledges and platforms everywhere. In a side room, Tom could see bins of dream stones, some white as slivers of the moon.

Ducking before anyone could see him, Tom went on until he came to an intersection that would lead to the treasure vault, but just as he was about to step into the corridor, he heard voices.

"Tell me it isn't so," Uncle Tumer was pleading. "I thought you were the Guardian's friend."

"What have you heard?" Mistral asked uncomfortably.

"Don't play innocent," Uncle Tumer snapped. "I know what you and he and the Grand Mage are doing. There's no secret a king can keep from his fool. I overheard him boasting that he's finally gotten you to help him steal the egg and wake the phoenix before its time. He's as mad as that monster, Vatten."

Tom sucked in his breath, hardly daring to believe his ears. In the silence, he waited for his friend to deny it, but she said softly, "The kingdom is being destroyed before our very eyes. There are no wiser creatures than our people. We will use the phoenix only against our enemies, and not against the world. What we do, we do for our people."

Tom stood in shock at his friend's treachery, but anger quickly replaced it. It was all he could do to keep from shouting at her.

"But you've prided yourself on your honor above everything else," the Fool protested. "Your friends trusted you, and yet you took the egg."

"I've found something that is more important than my honor," Mistral insisted, "the survival of dragonkind."

"You mustn't steal even for that," Uncle Tumer said.

"How dare you lecture me on what's right and what's wrong," Mistral said angrily.

"I am simply speaking the truth to you," Uncle Tumer pleaded, "as you once spoke to the king long ago. Or was . . . was this your plan all the time?" he asked.

"What do you take me for?" Mistral demanded. "It was the king's from the first moment he heard Hu wanted to enter the kingdom. But it was never mine. My only thought was for the safety of the phoenix and his Guardian."

"I thought he seemed eager on that first day to take it into the vault. These are terrible times when dragons are so twisted by fear that they think like that monster, Vatten." Uncle Tumer shook his head. "And so when the Guardian insisted on keeping the egg with him, His Highness needed you to switch an imitation for the real one."

"I resisted the idea as long as I could," Mistral said stiffly, "even though all I heard was one woe after another within the kingdom."

No wonder she had returned so tired and irritable from the war councils, Tom thought. The Dragon King and the others must have all been using guilt to force her to steal the egg.

"I thought your conscience was impregnable," Uncle Tumer said.

"So did I," Mistral admitted, "but then the Nameless One attacked this very palace. If the palace is not safe, what is? It made me realize just what tight straits we dragons are in. We have to force the phoenix to hatch."

Had Tom underestimated what her homeland meant to Mistral? Was she willing to sacrifice everything for it—even her friends?

"It's still not too late," Uncle Tumer begged. "Return the egg to the Guardian and restore your honor."

Mistral's voice took on a dangerous edge. "What's honor when we're fighting for our very race? But I wouldn't expect a coward like you to understand."

"Wait!" Uncle Tumer called forlornly.

"Do not vex me anymore, Fool! I will not allow dragonkind to disappear."

Mistral's angry voice sounded very close now. Tom

hastily ducked into a crevice. The coral worms scraped him as he squeezed in tight and a furious Mistral swam by. Uncle Tumer passed a moment later, pausing in front of the hidden boy, but the Fool was so lost in his gloomy thoughts that he looked neither to his left nor his right. Lowering his head with a sad jingle, the dragon gave a kick that propelled him through the water.

When he was gone, the boy slipped out again and peeked into the other corridor, but Mistral was gone as well. A moment later, he heard a heavy door thud shut.

Tom hated to be lied to, and he hated even more when it was a friend who was doing it. His blood pounded through his temples as the anger bubbled up inside him. Was this how Mr. Hu felt before he went wild in battle? Maybe Mistral and Monkey were right and the tiger's blood really was affecting him after all.

He gave a jump when he heard a small voice whisper in his ear. "It's safe to leave. She's gone into the vault." It was one of the tiny fake sea horses.

If Tom had a tail, he would have been lashing it back and forth. "Then"—the growl came from deep in his chest—"we have to get into the vault and see what they're up to."

CHAPTER NINE

Sidney was just as furious when Tom got back to Mr. Hu's room. "So that's why the king welcomed us all with open paws," the rat said, stamping a hind one. "He wanted the phoenix from the very start."

"For some, his paws were less open," Monkey grumbled as he folded his legs. "After pretending to be so high-minded and making me take an oath, he's the one who's the thief."

Tom pounced upon a pillow and began to punch it. "And Mistral helped him. I thought she was better than that."

They were both surprised when Monkey said, "Sometimes there is no clear-cut path for honor, and in her case, she must be torn: Does she keep faith with us, her friends, or with her people?"

Tom flung the pillow against the wall where it burst,

spreading kelp around the room. "You're defending her? But you're always teasing her."

"I tease her because I like her." Monkey plucked a bit of kelp from his fur. "I know what a hard, lonely road she's taken because I've traveled it myself." He pursed his lips. "But if both Mistral and the king are lying to us, I wonder if the healer is as well?"

Tom clenched his hands as he followed the ape's logic. "So they could keep Mr. Hu asleep while they stole the egg?"

"The dragons think he's the only one who can tell the true egg from the fake one. But they didn't figure on you. Dream stones have to be in physical contact with the dreamer to have an effect, so let's see what happens to Hu without it." Monkey found a piece of dragon silk and carefully removed the dream stone from the tiger's paw. Almost immediately, Mr. Hu gave a moan.

"Maybe we should put it back," Tom said, worried for the Guardian.

"Good dreams can be as powerful as any drug," Monkey said, wrapping up the stone carefully and hiding it beneath a cushion in a faraway corner.

Tom watched the tiger anxiously, but Mr. Hu fell back into an uneasy slumber. He was going to ask Monkey what he meant about dreams, but then he remembered the strange chamber. "When I was following the Grand Mage, I saw this room filled with dream stones and sleeping dragons." Tom described it briefly as he tucked the covers back around the elderly tiger.

Monkey scratched his jowls. "Well, this is just a guess, but I'd say it's like a hospital."

"But why so far below?" Tom asked. "It's like they want to keep it a secret."

Monkey folded his arms and let his chin sink to his chest while he thought. "If dragons have one weakness, it's dreaming. They live for centuries, and when they grow old, it becomes harder and harder to tell the waking world from their dreams. That might be a place for the dragons to rest."

"But some of the dragons didn't seem very old," Tom said.

"There are probably some dragons who simply prefer to retreat into dreams," Monkey said. "When times are horrible, dreams are kinder."

"Is that because of the war too?" Tom asked, feeling troubled.

"Maybe." Monkey nodded. "The dragons would consider it a shameful thing, so they would keep their young dreamers hidden."

"What if the healer comes by?" Sidney fretted, glancing at the cushion.

"Have no fear." With a flourish, Monkey plucked a hair from his tail and changed it into an exact replica of the dream stone, which he placed in Mr. Hu's paw. "Confidentially, I've found that dragons aren't as smart as they think they are. Oh, they know a lot of facts. If you want to know what a king ate for lunch a thousand years ago, they'll tell you. But when it comes to seeing through a little trick like this, they're hopeless." He rested his chin on a paw. "Now, just how are we going to get you inside that vault to switch the fake one for the real phoenix?"

At first, Tom thought the ape was making one of his usual jokes—and a rather unfunny one at that—until he saw that for once Monkey was serious.

"Me?" Tom asked, cradling the strange rose in his hands. "You're the one who should go. You've done it before, when you stole the staff."

"Since the king has broken every law of hospitality, my oath no longer binds me," Monkey said, motioning to his body. "But that doesn't change the fact that the dragons want to know where I and Hu are at all times. Now that we know how treacherous the dragons are, I should stay here to protect Hu. And you're the only one who can positively identify the rose."

Tom felt as though Monkey had dropped a boulder upon his shoulders. "But the dragons don't care where I am because they think I'm harmless," Tom said, his voice falling. He'd been counting on Monkey, who had a talent for thievery.

"It wouldn't be the first time the dragons would be wrong." The ape nudged him with a chuckle.

"You can't send the kid to do that," Sidney said with a

shiver that made all his fur quiver. "What if the king caught him? What do dragons do to thieves?"

Monkey laced his paws behind his head. "Technically, he'd be a spy. I'd be the thief."

"Thief or spy, there's nothing like a dragon when it comes to revenge," Sidney said, and drew a claw across his throat. "It won't be fun whatever they do."

"It can't be worse than tackling the Nameless One all by yourself," Monkey pointed out, then set his paws on the boy's shoulders. "Hu wouldn't have picked you as his apprentice if he didn't think you could handle this, Tom. Don't underestimate yourself. He saw something in you. And so do I. You have the heart of a Guardian, if not all the skills yet."

Tom had managed to distract the Nameless One, but was he up to challenging the whole dragon kingdom? Still, as bad as things were, the mouse Guardian, Surefoot, had faced even greater odds than this. He realized that Mr. Hu and Mistral were only half right: It may not matter what most people think of you, but it is important what your friends do.

As he tried to think of what to do, Tom began to scratch his cheek and felt the scale that the strange and powerful Empress had placed there.

He turned to a mirror to look at her mark. The golden scale winked in the light of a passing jellyfish lamp, its edges gleaming like needle-thin rainbows.

"You told me I could summon the Empress with this," Tom said, staring at it.

"Believe me," Sidney said with such a shudder that even his slender pink fingers trembled. "You don't want to meet her again."

Monkey simply said, "I think when she gave it to you, she meant you could only call upon her once. Do you really feel this is the time?"

"Don't you?" Tom asked, exasperated.

Monkey shrugged. "That's not for me to say. You're the Guardian while Mr. Hu is recovering."

Tom swallowed. After everything he had heard from the others, and especially after what the Grand Mage had told him about the Empress, he was not sure he wanted her help. He would have to be desperate to do that. He turned away from the mirror.

"Then I guess it's up to me," he said quietly. "How did you get into the vault?"

Sidney got off the bench. "Are you sure about this?"

Tom remembered what Mr. Hu had said about Mistral deciding to face death by ending her exile. "Mr. Hu warned me I'd have to make hard choices," he explained. "My grandmother did that, and so has he."

Monkey told him how he had done it, and then folded his arms. "Well, unfortunately the vault I broke into was in a different palace. And I'm sure the dragons would have taken precautions against a similar attempt here."

Perhaps Mistral had known that and so had felt safe to steal the rose. Tom felt even more furious at his former friend. "This is all Mistral's fault," he muttered. "Mr. Hu trusted her. So did I. How could she?" He felt a tigerish rage build inside him again until he thought he was going to explode. He tried to fight it but couldn't, and he began to prowl back and forth to work off some of the energy.

Sidney barely snatched his tail out of the way of Tom's foot. "You're almost as dangerous as Mr. Hu when he paces."

"Don't exaggerate," Tom growled.

Sidney edged away nervously. "Then why are you showing your teeth?"

The boy realized then that he had opened his mouth as if exposing fangs. Hastily he pressed his lips together.

With a skip and a hop, Monkey caught up with him, peering at Tom's face. "And this time you really have a little of that fiery glint in your eyes that Hu has."

"Will you stop with the stupid jokes?" Tom roared as he shoved Monkey away. "I'm still me." But the blood was pounding through his head now. How much of it was the tiger's and how much was his own? Mistral had called him a mongrel. Worse, she had lied to him and treated him like a fool. She didn't think he could do anything. Well, he would show her she was wrong: He was worthy to be a Guardian.

He wanted to strike at her and every other dragon in the kingdom. Though he had never had much patience before as a human, he felt even less of it now. All he could think about was how he'd like to crush the dragons and their palace.

Then, in the midst of his growing rage, he heard the voice of his grandmother whispering to him that his wits, rather than brute force, were the only way into the dragon's treasure vault.

He caught sight of where the dream stone in its wrapper pushed up the cushion slightly. Suddenly he had an idea of how he could steal back the phoenix egg.

Rounding on his heel, he sent jellyfish lamps swirling around in the current as he took the dream stone from its hiding place. "Could you pound this into powder?"

"Of course," Monkey said, taking the needle from behind his ear and expanding it to his staff. "But what do we do about the noise?"

"Bang it in rhythm, and Sidney and I will sing and dance," Tom said. He still felt excited, but it was under control now—as if it were raw energy being channeled into a pipe.

As Sidney floated overhead, he put a paw beneath his throat. "But I can't do either."

"All the better," Tom said, stamping his feet and singing both loudly and off-key. Looking slightly embarrassed, the rat settled on the floor and joined in, thumping his paws on the floor and mangling a tune at the top of his lungs.

Monkey crushed the dream stone in time to their song.

Fortunately for everyone's ears, it didn't take long. Then Tom explained his scheme, waiting for them to find fault with it, as he was sure they would.

To the boy's relief, Sidney clapped his paws together with a whistle of approval. "Not bad."

And Monkey bowed respectfully. "You've got a talent for thievery. If you ever want to become my apprentice rather than Hu's," Monkey offered with a wink, "I'd be glad to have you."

Then Monkey changed more hairs into little sea horses and had them all tear a bit of cloth from a rag and wrap up some of the powder. Soon he was surrounded by a cloud of them, each with a bit of dream dust.

Picking up the fake rose from the table, Monkey handed it to Tom. "Take this with you and exchange it for the real rose if you can. But remember: Don't take any unnecessary risks. If you don't think you can handle the theft, leave it to me." Then he replaced the rose with a second fake made from a hair on his tail. "Good luck to you and Sidney."

"Me?" Sidney squeaked in alarm.

Monkey gave him a little shake. "You wouldn't want him to go in alone, would you?"

The rat shuffled a hind paw back and forth while he thought about it. "Well, no."

"I'll be with you in a way," Monkey said, indicating the school of disguised little apes.

As Tom and Sidney left, the tiny fake sea horses spread

out loosely so that they were hardly noticeable in the marine snow that floated in the corridor.

"Making another deal?" the sentry teased Sidney.

"I'm going to make the biggest one yet," the rat said with a wink.

Tom and Sidney made their way as unobtrusively as they could down to the vault, but when Tom pointed out the dream chamber he had seen before, Sidney motioned to wait. "Stay here, will you? I'll be back in a jiff."

Before Tom could ask what he was doing, Sidney had slipped inside. The boy spent anxious moments waiting in the hallway until the rat returned, humming a little tune. "You never know when dream stones will come in handy," he said, very pleased with himself.

As they neared the vault, Tom heard the small voice of a sea horse whisper in his ear. "The High King and Mistral have left. There's just the Grand Mage inside."

"Good," Tom said. Taking a breath, he swam out into the hallway. The massive vault door was twice the boy's height and its bronze was green with age and looked as heavy as an automobile. A giant could not have battered it down, and Tom wondered how huge was the hoard it protected.

Tom thumped on it with a fist, listening to the echo boom from within. "Let us in."

The guard's answer was muffled by the thick doors. "I'm not supposed to open the vault to anyone."

"The chamberlain told us to put these jewels into the vault for safekeeping," Tom said, trying to sound bored. "I'll just leave them here and you can explain it to the chamberlain if they're missing."

Sidney was already scooting around the corner as Tom hurried after him. Behind them he could hear the click of a key turning in a lock, and he barely ducked out of sight before the door opened with a groan.

"Okay, it's safe," a sea horse said in his ear after an anxious moment.

When Tom risked peeking, he saw a dragon sprawled across the threshold of the vault. "That was quick work."

"The dust works faster when you take it inside the nostrils," the tiny sea horse said smugly.

When Tom entered the vault, he had to squint because of the glare. There were only a few of the jellyfish lamps floating about, but there was so much gold that it reflected the light everywhere. There were cups and bowls and vases and shining coins, some a thousand years old or more but looking as if they were newly minted. Bracelets and necklaces were draped around golden statues as well.

"Ooo." Sidney's paws twitched as they stretched forward eagerly.

Tom saw the giant anemones on either side of the doorway, up the sides, and even on the ceiling. Tentacles began to reach out. And a cloud of small purple jellyfish darted toward them.

"Stop that," Tom said, pulling Sidney back.

Instantly the anemones retracted their tentacles so that they looked like giant rainbow-colored lumps of dough, and the purple jellyfish disappeared into the shadows of the high ceiling.

"I bet you'd be dead in an instant if one of them stung you," Tom warned. "And there are other traps."

"So it's look but don't touch." Sidney sighed quietly. "You didn't tell me this was going to be such torture."

Deeper into the vault, the dragons kept their gems. Open jars were filled with rubies and diamonds and emeralds. More chests lay stacked against the wall, but the wood had rotted on some, leaking crowns and jewelry down the sides. The pearls, however, were most impressive. They came in bins, the smallest the size of marbles and ranging all the way to softballs. Some were loose, but others had been strung for storage and hung from the ceiling in gleaming, iridescent ropes.

"If that other palace vault was like this one, why'd Monkey only take the staff?" Sidney said disapprovingly. "I've got to have a talk with him."

The vault continued on and on until its end was lost to sight. The dragons had had thousands of years to gather their treasures.

"Where do we start looking for the egg?" Tom asked helplessly.

"Over here," a voice whispered.

The tiny sea horses guided them down an aisle to another, smaller chamber. The door was open, revealing mirrors and cauldrons and other magical implements. The tingling at the back of Tom's neck had grown to an itch, so he knew there was powerful magic here.

The Grand Mage lay curled up on the floor like a cat, smiling as if he were having the pleasantest of dreams. The dream dust apparently worked well on any size.

It was a shame that with all the Lore packed into the Grand Mage's brain there hadn't been room for ethics—but, as Monkey had observed, dragons might know a good many facts but that did not make them wise. Still, even if the elderly dragon had helped to steal the phoenix, he had been kind to Tom in other things and had taken a true scholar's pleasure in teaching him. The boy had come to like his teacher in spite of everything. Finding a bolt of gold cloth for a pillow, he set the dragon's head upon it.

The rose itself lay upon a small, high golden table. Strange patterns and runes had been painted on the table-top and streams of blue oil floated over the sides of a bowl hanging above it to bathe the rose.

"Is there anyone as clever as us?" a sea horse boasted.

"Or as bold?" another asked.

"Or daring?" a third said.

"No, no one," Tom responded as he crossed to the table and picked up the rose. It had always felt cool as stone before, but now it was warm to his fingers. As he stared, the red petals grew transparent and he saw a flashing shape floating within. "This is the real one," he said, and quickly substituted the fake. When he had stowed the rose in the pouch about his neck, he still felt its warmth.

As they left, the rat could not help looking from side to side, his paws beginning to twitch again. "Maybe just a souvenir."

"We've got what we came for," Tom said sternly, grabbing hold of his shoulder and steering him toward the vault door.

Sidney twisted around so he could stare longingly at a ruby the size of the boy's fist and then squinted at Tom, annoyed. "You know, you're getting to be as much of a killjoy as Mr. H."

Tom touched the rose within the pouch. "Well, I'm his apprentice, after all."

CHAPTER TEN

After they had pulled the door to the vault shut, Tom, Sidney, and the little sea horses hurried back to their rooms. Hardly able to believe what he'd accomplished, the boy darted through the water with strong, contented strokes.

"Why are you humming?" Sidney asked as they swam along.

"Am I?" Tom asked in surprise.

The rat eyed him. "Yeah, from deep in your chest. Maybe that's as close as humans can get to purring."

"I wish you and Monkey would stop with the jokes," he grumbled.

Mr. Hu had still not woken up when they returned. "He's been twitching," Monkey said, "so he must be waking up."

"No, no," Mr. Hu murmured, and stirred beneath the bedclothes.

As Tom carefully slipped the egg from the pouch around his neck, Monkey glanced at it. "Is it the real one?"

"Yes," Tom said, "but we can only be sure if Mr. Hu looks at it."

Monkey motioned the boy away. "Drastic times call for drastic measures."

Tom took a few steps from the bed. "What are you going to do?" he asked uneasily.

"You'll need to go much farther back." Monkey pointed. "Over there, behind the chaise lounge."

"You're not going to hurt Mr. Hu?" Tom asked, ready to defend the Guardian.

"More like the other way around." Monkey rolled up his sleeves.

Tom joined Sidney, who was already hiding behind the chaise lounge. "There's never a dull moment with the two of you around, is there?" the rat muttered.

Climbing onto the bed, Monkey hunched like a cat hunting a bird. When Mr. Hu rolled onto his back, Monkey pounced, wrapping his arms around the tiger's jaw so that he hugged it tight. Then he clapped both paws over the tiger's nostrils.

Sidney squatted down, squeezing his eyes shut. "Monkey's done some reckless things, but I never knew he wanted to become tiger chow."

"Mr. Hu won't be able to breathe," Tom said, starting to move around the chaise lounge.

The helpless Guardian gave a muffled, surprised whuff and then began to buck like a wild horse. As Monkey held on grimly, he panted. "I'd say . . . he's gotten . . . back all . . . his old energy."

Suddenly the tiger's eyes jerked open and he sat bolt upright, throwing Monkey off the bed. "You fool ape, what are you trying to do?" he gasped.

Monkey somersaulted neatly onto his hind paws. "Acting like an alarm clock. You've slept far too long, old friend."

Mr. Hu blinked his eyes irritably. "I'm still sleepy."

"That's the aftereffects of the dream stone," Monkey explained.

"Yes, the dream stone." The tiger's claws twitched and he glanced down at his empty paw before he began to search the bed. "Where is it?" he hissed, making a noise like giant scorpions skittering along a dusty floor.

Tom crossed the room to the tiger. "The dragons were keeping you unconscious even though you'd recovered."

"Such sweet dreams," Mr. Hu muttered as he began to toss the bedclothes about, hunting for the stone.

"The time for dreaming is over, Guardian," Monkey said, folding his arms.

Mr. Hu drew his lips back in a snarl. "Thief, did you steal my dream stone?"

"Stay away from him, Tom," Monkey warned, never taking his eyes off Mr. Hu. "I told you the dream stones are addictive if you misuse them." His voice became sweet and soothing as he spoke to the tiger. "The dragons put a fake rose here and stole the real one. They were going to wake the phoenix. But Tom and Sidney got it back."

Tom took the rose out of the pouch. "Can you tell us if this is the real one?"

He watched uneasily as the tiger rose stiffly on all fours and sniffed at it. "Yes, it's the phoenix. You were stupid to lose it in the first place. Don't let it out of your sight again," he growled, and then exposed his fangs at the ape. "Now give me back the dream stone."

Monkey slipped his staff, reduced to the size of a needle, from behind his ear. "Sorry, old boy. Nappy time is over. We have to leave."

"Give me the stone!" Mr. Hu roared, crouching, ears flattened, ready to pounce. His great voice resonated in the small room as powerful muscles stretched the shoulders of his sleeping gown. Claws shot out of his paws, ripping the mattress so that bits of seaweed floated loose.

It frightened Tom every time Mr. Hu slid into wildness. The gentleman he loved and respected vanished to be replaced by a mindless killing machine. Low growls rumbled from deep in the tiger's throat and his pink nostrils drew and expelled deep breaths that stirred the water so that the room vibrated as from the revving engine of a tank; and Tom knew that his master could be just as powerful and destructive as one.

The last thing the boy wanted to do was to call the

tiger's attention to him, but, he decided reluctantly, the duty came with being an apprentice. "Mr. Hu," he called sharply, and his heart skipped a beat when the tiger turned toward the boy. His snarling mouth had twisted his orange-and-black striped face into a terrifying mask. There was no recognition in the amber eyes, which had narrowed into slits, only anger and need.

Tom swallowed and went on. "My grandmother asked you to protect the phoenix."

The name made the tiger lift his head. "Mistress Lee," he murmured.

The tiger had been his grandmother's apprentice at one time, and he still revered her memory. "Yes," Tom pressed, "if she were here, she wouldn't like what you were doing. She gave it to you to protect."

Mr. Hu's jowls twitched as he fought to control himself. To Tom's relief, the tiger's ears began to rise, and he slowly lowered his haunches so that he was sitting. "Of course. I . . . I musn't be selfish. I must think of the rose first."

"That's right," Tom said gently as he stowed the rose back in the pouch. "We have to go before the dragons discover we've made the switch. They want the rose so badly, who knows what they'll do next?"

"We should never have left my store," Mr. Hu said. "It was too much of a temptation for the poor dragons, as it would be for any creature, no matter how good." He tried to climb off the bed but stumbled. Tom had to use both hands to support him. "Still so groggy though."

"You've been under the spell of the dream stone for a whole month," Monkey assured him. "You'll wake up after a while."

"But will the dragons give us that time?" Mr. Hu said grimly. With Tom's help, he got up.

"Well, let's not wait around to find out," Monkey said, and transformed himself into a compact but muscular dragon. "Ugh." He frowned as he examined a foreleg. "Why would anyone wear scales if they could have fur as lovely as mine?"

"Are you up to changing the rest of us, Mr. H.?" Sidney asked the tiger.

The tiger blinked his eyes groggily. "It's still a little hard for me to concentrate on all the intricacies, but perhaps if I have Master Thomas's help."

Tom hesitated as he took Mr. Hu's suit and hat from the wardrobe. "The Grand Mage taught me a few basics about transformation," he said in a low voice. "Maybe I could help a little."

Mr. Hu scratched his muzzle. "You continued your magic lessons? Excellent, but when we get a chance, we'll have to have a little test to make sure you learned the correct way to do things." By the "correct" way, Tom knew that Mr. Hu meant *his* way rather than the dragons'.

The tiger seemed pleased when he saw the condition

of his clothes. "You took care of my things," he said.

"Almost as well as he took care of you," Sidney said.

Mr. Hu beamed at his apprentice. "You've even gotten to look more like a tiger cub while I've been asleep."

"Don't you think we should concentrate on escaping the palace instead of making jokes?" Tom complained, and nudged Sidney. "I think we'll need more dream dust. It's a good thing that you took some dream stones from that room."

The scandalized rat clutched his paws against his fur where they were stored. "But they're merchandise!"

"Sidney," Monkey scolded as he changed all his hairs, disguised as scales now, into tiny sea horses that happily joined their brothers.

"Okay, okay." Sidney sighed. "But you're breaking my heart." He took out a cloth bundle. When he unwrapped it and set it on the floor, they saw half a dozen small stones.

With his staff, Monkey crushed all of Sidney's stock. Wincing at every blow, the rat stamped his feet and howled out a mournful song that was truly heartfelt. At the same time, while Tom helped Mr. Hu to dress, the boy told him briefly what had happened during his long slumber. The tiger looked sad rather than angry at Mistral's treachery.

"Aren't you mad?" Tom asked.

The tiger shook his head as he adjusted the red handkerchief in the breast pocket of his suit. "She has sacrificed much. It's no wonder she's finally succumbed."

"It's almost as if the phoenix egg had a curse," Tom said. "We came here to be safe, and it turned out to be the most dangerous place so far."

"The phoenix is blameless," Mr. Hu scolded gently. "It's Vatten and his lust for power that drove us here. He can instill a fear more destructive than his monsters because it poisons friendship and transforms friends into enemies." He smiled at his apprentice. "But you haven't disappointed me, Master Thomas. You filled in ably for me when I was incapacitated."

"I'm glad you can take over again," Tom said, turning red. "I let Mistral steal the egg." Taking the pouch from around his neck, he tried to return it to the Guardian.

Mr. Hu held up a paw. "And you realized it and got it back. You've earned the right to bear it."

As much as the boy tried to give the phoenix egg to the tiger, the tiger was just as firm on the boy wearing it, until Tom finally put it around his neck again.

When Monkey had finished crushing the stones into a small pile of dust, Sidney plopped down on the floor and massaged a hind paw. "My tootsies are sore," the rat complained.

"We'll wish we had more dust before we're done," Monkey said, motioning to the swirling cloud of fake sea horses.

Mr. Hu was gazing at the tiny heap as if he longed to

scoop it up. Tom got ready to throw himself at the tiger, but fighting his own desire, Mr. Hu tore his eyes away. "Never again," he swore as the cloud swarmed over the dust until nothing remained.

While Monkey stood guard, the tiger sat on his haunches and talked over the transformation spell with Tom. As Tom suspected, his knowledge was still rudimentary compared to the Guardian's, but Mr. Hu decided that if Tom could help with the simple things, then he could tackle the more difficult parts, such as the manual signs. The magic spell, as Mr. Hu worked it out, would be like a duet, with Tom handling a simple chorus and the tiger providing a chant, like the bass notes in a song.

Under the tiger's guidance, Tom drew diagrams on the floor and then he, Mr. Hu, and Sidney took their places. Closing his eyes, Tom did his best to remember everything the Grand Mage had taught him, especially about concentrating. He didn't want to turn anyone pink this time.

He felt more relief than triumph when he opened his eyes and found himself staring at a pair of dragons armored like warriors.

"Well done, Master Thomas," said the dragon with the amber eyes. "You haven't wasted your time learning Dragon Lore."

Tom glanced down at himself and saw the scales across his belly. He was a dragon too—and not a pink one, for which he was grateful.

The other dragon was smaller, with yellowish scales. "I wouldn't mind keeping this baby when you change me back," Sidney said as he swished his tail back and forth. "What a weapon."

"You'd keep tripping over something that big," the tiger said.

"How are you feeling?" Tom asked. Though he had played a small part in the spell, he was feeling tired himself.

Mr. Hu wriggled his shoulders. "I feel as fit as a fiddle after that long sleep. Now let's try out some of that dream dust on the guard outside."

Opening the door a crack, Monkey sent out a few of the tiny sea horses. It only took a moment to render the sentry unconscious and for the ape to drag him inside. At his master's orders, Tom helped Mr. Hu transform the dragon into the tiger's own image. Once they'd put him in the bed, they changed a cushion into an imitation dream stone, which they put in the guard's paw. Then he transformed another cushion into an imitation flower.

"This might buy us a little more time to escape. The dragons know you won't leave without me, and if they think I'm still in bed, they'll be searching the palace." Mr. Hu wiped his forehead with a paw. "I suppose the best route out of the palace is through the main entrance."

"Mr. H., it'd be better to use an exit where there aren't any guards." Sidney gave a cough. "You know how we rats are. We like to explore. I found corridors that the dragons haven't used in centuries. The coral's so overgrown, it'd be a tight squeeze for a normal-sized dragon and I bet they never use them. One leads through a side gate into the gardens. I could see through the keyhole, but it's locked."

"Leave the gate to me," Monkey said, slapping the rat on the back. "Sidney, you're a gem."

"I'd prefer some real ones from the vault." Sidney sighed.

"What are trinkets compared to helping friends?" Monkey teased him.

"You can't hang friends around your neck," Sidney said, but the rat was too cheerful to stay glum for long. "I say let's blow this joint and get a decent burger."

They began to make their way down through the great palace. Fortunately their disguises fooled everyone they met. Dragon and servant alike simply hurried by them without a glance, and the lower they went, the fewer they met of any class.

"How much farther?" Mr. Hu asked.

"It's not very far," Sidney urged, and began to kick for all he was worth. The rat dove for another hundred meters before he announced, "Right here." With a flip, the rat headed into a corridor. "Yipes! It's the cops!"

"Children," Monkey said, pointing with his paw to the sea horses, and the cloud of dream-dust–carrying creatures began to move forward.

Tom flung up his own paw when he heard the jingling of tail bells. "Wait." And at a signal from Monkey, the sea horses halted.

As they joined Sidney in the corridor, they found it was Uncle Tumer. "When I saw Tom and the rat come out of the vault, I figured out what you were up to," Uncle Tumer said. "I came here to wait for you. A jester has to have an escape route, in case he tries the king's patience once too often, and I've spent long hours exploring the palace. I thought you'd come this way."

"So you're going to turn us in to gain the king's favor," Monkey said.

Uncle Tumer lifted his head with a defiant chiming. "I'm tired of waiting on that fat worm."

"I thought you were afraid of dying," Tom said.

"I've been dying a bit every day that I've played the fool," Uncle Tumer said softly, "but the worst was when I abandoned Mistral and Tom rather than face the Nameless One together. I would do anything not to endure that misery. Please let me guide you to the upper realms."

"Some would say you're even more of a fool to join us," Monkey warned.

"No, I was a fool long ago when I abandoned honor for safety," Uncle Tumer confessed. "What I did shamed my family, but what the king and Mistral are doing shames all dragonkind. If the royal fool can tarnish dragonkind's honor, then it's up to his lowly fool to restore it. A coward can find courage and a fool can tell the truth." The dragon bowed his head first to Tom and then to Sidney. "It took a gasser and a rat to teach the dragons a lesson about true courage and honor."

"Us?" Tom asked, astounded.

"Didn't you take on all the dragons almost by yourself?" Uncle Tumer demanded. "Please, let me come with you."

Tom floated uncomfortably, unused to being asked a favor by anyone. He glanced for help at Mr. Hu, who was circling around the dragon slowly.

"Are you sure you want to do this?" the Guardian asked.

Twisting his tail around, Uncle Tumer ripped off the bells and flung them away. Then, seizing the ribbonfish, he yanked them from his head and sent them after the bells. The stunned fish fell for a moment and then recovered to dart away like rainbow-colored arrows. "Uncle Tumer is no more. I'm Ring Neck again."

Sidney eyed Ring Neck suspiciously. "Why should we trust you?"

"I don't blame you for thinking all dragons are treacherous after this betrayal," Ring Neck said humbly, "but I swear on my father's grave that I tell the truth."

Mr. Hu turned to Tom. "What do you think, Master Thomas?"

Tom hesitated, surprised at being consulted.

"Master Thomas, I need your counsel now, not your obedience," Mr. Hu said. "You espied the high king's trick and won back the phoenix. You proved yourself a worthy successor."

As Tom studied the dragon, there was something in his desperate eyes that reminded the boy of himself. When Tom had faced the Nameless One, it had not been because he was brave but because he wanted to imitate past Guardians. He sensed that Ring Neck was just as hungry to live up to his father's bravery. "I think he's okay."

"Then," Mr. Hu said as he stretched out a scaled paw, "we'll be glad of your company."

"Humph," the rat sniffed. "Some people never learn."

"Take this," Ring Neck said, holding out a brass key. "I hunted all over this palace for the key to that gate and I've been saving it for just such a moment."

The rat gave the dragon a skeptical look, took the key, and swam into a narrow opening in the wall. Tom managed to slip in after him and saw that the dragons had let the coral overgrow this corridor, which had been reduced to a thin tunnel.

"Blast it! I'm stuck," Mr. Hu panted from behind him.

"Monkey, you push from outside," Tom said as he grasped the Guardian's paws.

"I think all your weight settled to your hips while you were asleep, Hu." Monkey grunted.

"The first part is the hardest," Ring Neck said.

"And how are you going to fit?" Tom called back to him.

"Fools must keep themselves small," Ring Neck said. "I know I'll get through. Or I'll shrink myself. Fools have no pride."

By desperate tugging and shoving, they managed to squeeze Mr. Hu into the passage, which widened a bit behind the entrance. Even the jellyfish lanterns had abandoned the place.

Holding on to the tip of Sidney's tail, Tom kept his other paw on Mr. Hu to guide him along in the darkness.

Though they all would have liked to go faster, the curving coral tunnel prevented it. The farther they went, the more Tom had the feeling they were being buried alive, and each had cuts and scrapes from the razorlike coral.

It seemed forever before Sidney told them they had reached the gardens. They felt a cold current as he opened the gate and swam outside. When Tom followed, he saw that they had emerged from a side gate screened by a group of coral-covered statues and ten-foot-long lacy sponges. High above, the palace towered over them. All around the edges of the gardens, flickering lights climbed upward through the dark water.

"Star rise," Tom murmured.

Mr. Hu pointed at the arch that gleamed in the reflected light of star rise. "We have to get to land as soon as we can, before they discover we've escaped."

"If Räv tracked us to the museum, Vatten's monsters could be waiting in ambush," Monkey reminded them. "We'd be running from one enemy straight into the paws of another."

"I only thought I saw her," Tom chipped in. "Maybe I didn't."

Mr. Hu smiled grimly. "We're between a rock and a hard place then: dragons or Vatten's creatures."

"If you try to fight your way across the dragon kingdom, you'll be captured for sure," Ring Neck warned.

"So it's an absolute certainty against a mere possibility," Mr. Hu grunted. "We'll have to chance the gate."

Monkey instructed the cloud of tiny monkeys hovering around. "Go ahead of us, children."

They swam low, just above the coral worms. A couple of times Tom fought giggling as the glowing tentacles tickled him. Though the group had the shapes of dragons, they did not automatically have the muscles. Soon Sidney and Tom were swimming clumsily, their bodies exhausted. Mr. Hu swam energetically but just as poorly because his muscles had grown weak with disuse after all that time in bed.

They were halfway across the gardens when an alarm gong reverberated below.

"They must have found the vault guard and the Grand Mage," Tom said.

"And tested the fake rose we left," Sidney added.

Other gongs began to answer above and below and around them until it seemed as if the entire palace were vibrating.

Monkey clapped his paws over his ears. "What was it the king said to me about dragons not letting go of a treasure once they had their paws on it?"

"Hopefully my double will fool them a little while longer and they'll be seeking you within the palace," Mr. Hu said.

A haughty voice called down to them, "Halt, who goes there?"

A squad of dragons floated overhead, their frilled, plumed bodies silhouetted against the bright surface.

"Just out for a little trip around the gardens." Monkey tried to sound cheerful.

After their rout by the Nameless One, the Imperial Guard seemed doubly determined to do their duty. "Everyone is to return to the palace to be searched," the sergeant said.

"Thanks, but we've had enough of scaly hospitality," Monkey said, and called to the cloud of tiny fake sea horses. "Now, children."

"Stay where you are." The dragons dove as one, wings and paws pulled in tight so that they looked like daggers with gleaming jade blades.

The sea horses rose like a pale mist that seemed far too fragile to halt the powerful squad, whose sharp fangs and steel claws tore the cloud into swirling ribbons.

Sidney nervously flexed his claws. Mr. Hu crouched in the water as if eager for revenge against the creatures who had tried to steal the phoenix. His enforced sleep had so rejuvenated him that he felt as energetic as a cub. Though not as confident as the Guardian, Tom took his place beside him. Monkey was the only one who floated unconcerned with his forelegs folded, humming to himself.

Tom watched in alarm as the dragons plunged toward them, their powerful, scaled bodies dropping like armored tanks—then he noticed that their eyes had closed.

"Out of the way!" Mr. Hu jerked him to the side as a dragon plummeted past.

The dragons landed within the gardens. The coral worms writhed and flashed around them while the warriors lay like slumbering hatchlings, apparently none the worse for their fall. With their frills and plumes, they blended so well into the gardens that Tom would have missed them if he hadn't seen exactly where they fell. The decorations, he thought, also made effective camouflage.

"What magic is this?" Ring Neck asked, then slapped one paw against another. "Ah, so you crushed a dream stone. You're really as clever as they say, Monkey."

The ape gave credit where it was due. "It was Tom's idea—again."

"Well done, Master Thomas," Mr. Hu said approvingly.

Tom felt his cheeks flush. At least he was proving the

Guardian a little right in choosing him.

The cloud of sea horses swarmed around Monkey, who restored them to his tail by the pawful. "But that was all the dream dust we had."

Sidney slapped his forehead. "I knew I should have taken more."

"Quickly," Mr. Hu said, "before anyone else notices the missing patrol."

They swam on faster, skimming over the gardens and over the edge into the glittering mist. As they descended, the glowing mist dissolved into swirling ribbons of light that seemed to flow from their very bodies.

This time Tom had a front-row seat for the star rise as the creatures rose hungrily toward the moon. Some were no bigger than pinpoints of light, but he made out fish whose sides flashed dots and stripes in some sign language all their own. Schools of squid jetted past in a swarm of fiery arrows. More sedate jellyfish drifted by them, their sides rippling like tasseled parasols.

When they reached the gate to the land, they found a squad of soldiers who were all staring at the palace. "What's going on?" the sergeant asked. Dragons were flitting all around the palace like flies.

"Trickery is more your field," Mr. Hu whispered to Monkey.

"There never was a dragon I couldn't fool." The disguised ape winked, then puffed himself up as importantly as he could. "We are on an important mission for the king himself." The ape knew how to imitate dragon courtiers, giving the guard his haughtiest glare. "Some of the prisoners have escaped. We must carry an urgent message to the upper realms."

The sergeant swept his paw up and down the back of his long neck. "Maybe I should make sure."

"Fool," Monkey snapped, "this can't wait. If you value your neck, you'll obey instantly."

Even so, the sergeant hesitated for a while, but in the end, Monkey's blustering worked. Finally the sergeant turned to one of his squad and said curtly, "Activate the gate."

Consulting a scroll, the guard began to draw a diagram. They waited anxiously while the guard drew in the sand, checking his book frequently and making corrections.

"This is *most* urgent," Monkey reminded him again.

"Yes, I heard you the first time," the harried guard snapped back as he checked the scroll again, "but we don't send many to the upper realms anymore, and I have to do it right or you could wind up at the wrong place."

Ring Neck, who had been keeping watch, whispered, "Someone's coming."

Mr. Hu's eyes narrowed and he growled, "It's Mistral." He craned his long neck so he could murmur to Monkey. "Keep those slugs at it while we deal with her."

"She's hard enough to have as a friend," Monkey said. "I hate to have her as an enemy."

CHAPTER ELEVEN

"Ring Neck, you stay with Monkey," Mr. Hu said.

The dragon raised a paw and pleaded, "I swore that I would get you home."

The former fool looked so desperate that Tom spoke up for him. "Please, Mr. Hu."

The tiger stared at the dragon. "Yes, well, Master Thomas knows you better than I do. Let's go."

"This is a big mistake," Sidney muttered to the Guardian, but the loyal rat started forward.

As they neared Mistral, Tom wondered if the four of them could handle a full-size dragon in the sea. He and Sidney couldn't do much, and Ring Neck was a professional fool, not a warrior. Mr. Hu might have recovered his energy, but his muscles were still flabby from lack of use.

"Ring Neck, what are you doing here?" Mistral demanded, halting as they drew close.

"Just out for a little swim with some friends." Ring Neck tried to sound as casual as he could.

Mistral counted them with her claws. "Three here and it looks like one more at the gate." As she scrutinized the transformations intently, Tom covered up the pouch about his neck. "The disguises are a decided improvement in your appearances," the dragon grunted smugly. "I'm assuming that you've returned the favor and fooled us with an imitation Hu, but those idiots haven't figured that out yet. They're still turning the palace upside down for the rest of you, but I figured I'd take a chance and wait for you here."

Mr. Hu crouched as he got ready to spring through the water. "I warn you. One shout and I'll rip out your throat."

Mistral squinted. "You must be Hu. Do you really think you can stop me, even if you've recovered your strength?"

"No, but perhaps the two of us can." Ring Neck raised a paw. "Leave, Tom. Take the rat with you."

"What's gotten into you?" Mistral asked.

"A coward can find courage and a fool can tell the truth," Ring Neck repeated, tensing.

"You always had a terrible sense of timing." Mistral chuckled. "Those virtues will be no more useful in the upper realms than they are in the sea."

Mr. Hu blinked in surprise. "Don't you want to take us back?"

"Only to your store," Mistral said, and glanced at Ring

Neck. "It took courage to tell me the truth. You were the wise one and I was the fool."

"But your land, your titles," Tom said. He knew what those had meant to her. "You're going to give up everything?"

"I give up nothing. They were never as important as friends." Mistral dipped her head to the boy and then to the others. "I'm sorry that it took this long for me to remember that."

Tom was still doubtful. "Are you willing to go into exile again?"

Ring Neck lifted his head. "But she won't be alone."

Mistral seemed suddenly embarrassed. "Is that what you want after what I've done?"

"Yes," Ring Neck insisted.

Mistral recovered her usual gruffness. "Humph, you'll have to do what I say. I'm the one who knows the way of the upper realms."

"You should've known she'd want to be the boss." Sidney nudged the former fool. "I'll sell you earplugs in your size cheap."

Mistral lowered her neck in a deep bow to Mr. Hu. "Guardian, I know I have cast aside the faith you once had in me, but I swear that I only wanted the safety of the phoenix when I agreed to come here. However, from the very first the king planned to steal the egg, and he made the Grand Mage, the healer, and myself forget our honor.

We all thought we were doing it for the greater good. Let me make amends. I promise I will never betray you again. I must have lost my senses temporarily."

The tiger still watched her warily, ready for a treacherous attack. "I've sacrificed much for my own clan. What would I have done if an entire race was at stake? But dragons are in as much danger as they ever were."

"I can't help what the other dragons do. I realize now I can only answer for myself." She looked at Ring Neck. "It took a good friend to remind me."

"I think you take on too much blame for the fall of dragonkind," Ring Neck said, drifting even closer, "but if you must feel guilty, at least let me share some of it."

"The knowledge of what is happening here will make exile even harder," Mistral said.

"I've been an outcast here," said Ring Neck, looking away. "Sea or land, it won't be an exile if we're together."

Mistral hovered for a moment. Faced with monsters, she had always been brave and decisive, but this was something new.

Ring Neck's long neck dipped in an elegant bow. "That is, if you'll have a coward and a fool."

Mistral glanced at the others and then back at Ring Neck. "You might have picked a time when we didn't have an audience," she said.

But as they swam back toward the gate, they spoke in low voices.

"Mistral looks happier than when she got her title," Tom whispered to Mr. Hu.

"If anyone has earned it, Mistral has," the tiger replied.

Monkey hid his surprise well when they joined him. "Her Grace will join us," Mr. Hu announced.

"What's the delay?" Mistral asked in her best duchess voice.

"I'm almost done," the harassed guard said, and under his breath he muttered, "I'm in just as much of a hurry to get rid of you as you are to leave."

As they waited impatiently, Mistral could not help sizing up Monkey. "Just how long are you?" she asked him softly.

"Long enough," Monkey said slyly.

"You've made yourself bigger than me, haven't you?" Mistral growled.

Monkey slung a foreleg around Mistral's shoulders. "What's pride among scaly friends?"

"Plenty," Mistral said, peering over her shoulder as she tried to compare lengths.

"More company," Sidney said, nodding behind them.

A dozen dragons were swimming their way.

"Tell us as soon as it's ready," Mistral said to Monkey.

As the arrivals neared, they saw it was a group of steel-shod warriors led by Tench, who gave a curt nod. "Your Grace, what a pleasant surprise to find you here."

"Shouldn't you be busy back at the palace, helping

with the search?" Mistral asked frostily.

Tench slowed as he drew closer. "His Highness is seeking you, and so I came to escort you back."

"I will see him shortly," Mistral lied.

Tench stretched out his neck to stare. "Is that Uncle Tumer? I hardly recognize you without your motley."

"I thought Her Grace was in need of amusement as much as His Highness," Ring Neck said quickly.

Behind them, Tom saw Monkey signal as the guard rose from the sand. "They're ready," he murmured.

Tench narrowed his eyes as he smiled at Mistral. "I knew you would fall again, traitor. I saw how you preened and strutted while worthier dragons toiled away in your shadow—but I knew it was a matter of time before you made another mistake. I'll redeem my reputation with your hide."

"Go through," Mistral said to Mr. Hu.

The tiger's warlike instincts were aroused. "We'll stay with you."

"Think of your mission." Mistral glared. "And think of him." She pointed her tail at Tom.

Mr. Hu stiffened as if it hurt his pride, but he nodded. "Yes, you're right."

"I never thought I'd hear you admit that," Mistral laughed. "Now I can die happy."

"Stop them," Tench commanded.

Ring Neck glided next to Mistral. "We've had little

time together, but it has been bliss."

"Being hunted?" Mistral asked. "You have a strange idea of entertainment, and yet this is the merriest I've been too."

"Pangolin, Pangolin!" Tench and his warriors yelled.

Mistral answered with her battle cry, "Kamsin, Kamsin!" and Ring Neck shouted, "Chukar!" And as he sped after her, the former jester seemed to shed all his years as a fool and become the duke he had once been.

The clash of dragons was an awesome sight. Huge muscled columns of armor and scales and fangs collided, and then the water was swirling and roiling as their bodies twisted and whirled, almost too fast to be seen.

"Master Thomas, come," Mr. Hu said, nudging the boy.

Reluctantly Tom swam toward the gate with the Guardian and Sidney.

"What's going on?" the sergeant demanded.

"A private little feud," Mr. Hu explained.

Tom couldn't resist looking back, but all he could see was a flurry of bubbles with the occasional flash of a steel-tipped claw.

"Now, Master Thomas," Mr. Hu said urgently, and pushed Tom through. As he stepped into the dry air within the empty tank, Tom felt as though his skin had caught fire and his lungs were aflame. Though he was disguised as a dragon, the original spell still affected him. He stood gasping in panic as the crab jumped up in surprise from in front of his television set.

"No one told me anyone was coming. Unannounced arrivals are illegal," the gatekeeper complained sourly. "Who are you?"

The ache in Tom's body and lungs eased the next instant. The rest of the breathing spell must have taken over.

Before the boy could answer, Sidney bulled into his back. The two of them fell into the room.

"How do you like that!" Sidney exclaimed, rolling off Tom. "That big lug was telling the truth about wanting to help us."

As Mr. Hu followed, the gatekeeper kept twisting his eyestalks so he could see both them and some late-night talk show.

"Is that all of you?" the gatekeeper asked, clicking his claws at them impatiently.

"I can see you're charming as ever." Mr. Hu helped Tom and Sidney to their feet. "There are three more."

Monkey plunged through a moment later, breathless. He turned, watching with the others. "They're giving as good as they get," he said.

"Keep that in mind before you tease her again," Mr. Hu said.

Monkey bit his lip, worried for his friend. "Let's just hope there is a next time."

They were all surprised when Mistral fell into the room

next, rolling head over tail into them. "That idiot," she snapped as they helped her up. "He shoved me through the gate."

"He wanted to save you," Monkey said. Suddenly he leaped past her, smashing his heavy dragon's tail against the mystic signs on the left wall.

The crab scuttled forward angrily. "What are you doing? No one can leave now!"

"And no one can come through until you get it repaired," Monkey said, holding off the outraged crab with a paw.

"You fool ape, what have you done? Ring Neck's back there," Mistral cried, springing upon Monkey.

It was all Monkey could do to keep Mistral from tearing out his throat. "Ring Neck told me to do that before I came through."

"He . . . what?" Mistral raised her head, stunned.

Monkey rolled away, feeling his neck to see if it was still intact. "He said it was the only way. He was going to keep his word no matter what."

"He got us back to the land," Tom said, remembering the dragon's oath.

"But what about me?" Mistral said, staring anxiously toward the now useless gate.

Mr. Hu crouched beside her. "He did this to save you too. I think you were as important to him as Master Thomas is to me."

Mistral reared up on her hind legs, bending her head back on her long neck. "That fool. That stupid, noble fool." Tears rolled down her sable cheeks and fell from high above like shining pearls.

CHAPTER TWELVE

The yen huo have fur all of black and bodies like beasts.
From their mouths, they spit fire.

—Shan Hai Ching

The chu chien have heads like humans but their ears are like
an ox's and they have only one eye. Their bodies resemble
leopards with long tails and they have powerful roars.

—Shan Hai Ching

The gatekeeper was beside himself with outrage because not only had Monkey destroyed the gate but, in his struggle with Mistral, he had also knocked over the television set and wrecked it as well. It took a couple of swats from Monkey's paws on his hard shell—which hurt Monkey more than the crab—to make him retreat into a corner. There he clicked his claws menacingly as curses bubbled from his mouth—none of which fazed the ape, who had heard such things often enough. The ape simply went about changing himself into his human shape, complete with dapper white suit.

"Your turn, Master Thomas," Mr. Hu said, folding his scaled forelegs.

Aware that his master was watching him intently, Tom worked out the spell and tried it. Though scales softened and paled into human skin, his neck was still as long as it was when he was a dragon. "I thought I was getting the hang of this magic stuff." He groaned.

"You've come a long way in a short time, but you can't expect to master it yet." Mr. Hu harrumphed. "In transformation spells, you must always pay attention to the basics first. You've got the texture right, but you've neglected the most basic fundamental of length." Mr. Hu helped restore Tom completely. When the tiger had resumed his human disguise, he began to fuss with his clothes.

"Mr. Hu," Tom whispered to him and pointed at Mistral.

She sat staring at the broken gate as if she were trying to figure out some way of repairing it and returning to the battle with Tench.

The tiger stopped worrying about his appearance and went over to his friend. "You have to transform now. We have to go."

"To what?" she demanded. "To wander by myself again? This second exile is even crueler. That fool should have let me die with him."

Sidney bounced up and down on his hind paws. "Before I took this little vacation, business was booming. If you don't want to live with them, you can always bunk with me behind the garbage cans. I could always use a partner—especially one with some muscle, if you know what I mean."

It was Monkey who understood Mistral best—perhaps

he could not have teased her so well otherwise.

"The king," he said as he waved his staff to keep the still sputtering crab in his corner, "would like nothing better than your death."

Blinking, Mistral roused from her misery. "The last thing I want to do is make that fat toad happy."

"Go on living just to spite that fat old worm," Monkey coaxed.

Mistral thought for a moment and then rose from the floor. "That would be the best revenge—to outlive that creature. He's brought shame to all the dragons." In the next instant, she had become a sad-looking woman in a shimmering black suit.

"Monkey," Mr. Hu said, "you'd better go first and scout around, just in case Master Thomas really did see Räv earlier."

"Right," the ape said. Opening the door, he glanced this way and that before he stepped outside. They shut it behind him, waiting until they heard a tap. "It's clear."

Sidney, now back in his rat form, was the first through the door and kissed the planks of the pier. "Home. If I ever touch as much as a glass of water, it'll be too soon."

"Spare us all and bathe sometimes," Monkey teased, giving Sidney's tail a good-natured tweak.

As Tom stepped outside onto the pier, he saw it was evening. The planks of the pier were slippery with the damp night air.

As soon as Mistral was through the door, the crab slammed it shut, almost catching the cuff of her suit. The next instant the little window at the top of the door opened and the crab's eyestalks thrust through the hole to glare at them. "And never come back!"

The only trouble was that there were no taxis in sight. As Monkey stood waiting to hail a cab, Tom looked at San Francisco. On that August evening, lights swept from the wharf area up the hills like a net. "I won't be able to see the city lights without thinking of star rise."

"San Francisco is pretty in the evening," Mistral agreed, "but it's only a poor imitation of what we saw in the ocean."

"It's about time you showed up," a very annoyed voice called from beneath them. Everyone gave a jump as Räv emerged from the right side of the pier, where she had been hidden on a perch beneath the planks.

Mr. Hu glared. "You!"

Räv blew irritably into her hands to warm them. "It's a pleasure to see you again too. I've been waiting for you to come out of the museum, and I've had a cold, miserable time of it! What kept you?"

"You fool ape," Mistral rasped, "didn't you look *under* the pier?"

Chagrined, Monkey pivoted as he reached behind his ear. "I'll make up for it now."

At the same time, Mistral and Mr. Hu placed themselves

on either side of Tom, readying for the avalanche of enemies. "You won't find us easy prey," the tiger growled.

Hastily Räv raised both hands in peace. "Please, relax.
I'm all alone." In the light from the streetlamps, her pale
hair floated around her foxish face like a ghost's. "I don't
mean you any harm. In fact, quite the opposite."

Mr. Hu frowned as he slipped the green rock from his
pocket. "How did you escape? I saw you drawn into this
with my own eyes."

Räv wagged an index finger from side to side like a
metronome. "You only thought you did, but as soon as I
saw the clay in your hand, I knew what it was for. I figured
you'd have to put some kind of filter into the spell or it
would have sucked up everything, including the sea and
the ocean." Räv walked confidently toward them, her arms
folded around herself for warmth. She stopped in front of
them. "So I heaped a layer of sand over me quick, and that
coating kept the trap from drawing me up with the hsieh.
I'd watched how you changed back to your regular size,
and once you were gone, I did that to myself."

"You're indeed very clever. So you've kept spying on us
all this time for Vatten." The mere mention of their enemy's
name made the tiger expose his fangs angrily.

Räv gazed up earnestly at Mr. Hu. "When Vatten left
me to die, I swore to serve him no more. If I still followed
him, you would be dead now."

Mistral seized her wrist. "Then perhaps you're trying

174

to steal the phoenix for yourself."

Räv twisted free. "This is no way to treat an ambassador from the rebels. I've brought you a proposal."

Skeptically Mr. Hu stowed the green rock back in his pocket. "And from what are you rebelling?"

The girl drew herself up as befitted an official representative. "There were many in the old Clan of the Nine who were sick of this endless war. It might have meant something to our ancestors who knew Kung Kung, but after thousands of years his cause has become meaningless. After I saw you go into the museum, I went home."

"And where's that?" Mr. Hu demanded sharply.

"In an area of San Francisco that you never suspected," she said, waving a hand vaguely. "And I learned that there's been open rebellion against Vatten. Many want to live our own lives now instead of mindlessly following him."

"I've heard rumors that there was some dissent among the Clan of the Nine." Mr. Hu stroked his little gray goatee gravely. "But why would anyone of his folk turn away from Vatten when he is at the height of his power?"

"We've learned of Vatten's plans if he can't regain the phoenix and rule the world," Räv said, shaking her head as if she still could not believe it. "He's going to carry out Kung Kung's original plan for vengeance."

The tiger sucked in his breath. "Destroy the world? How?"

"We don't know, but we're done following that madman," Räv insisted as she straightened her clothes, "and we'll join with anyone who's willing to stop him—even with our traditional enemies."

"You mean the dragons?" Tom asked.

"Yes," Räv said.

Mr. Hu gestured toward the west. "And there are also warriors, spirits, and the many others who have fought the Clan of the Nine."

"Maybe they're ready for peace too," she said. "Maybe they'll make a truce and join us. We have a common foe now—Vatten."

Monkey, Mistral, and Sidney seemed equally surprised. From what little history he had learned, Tom knew that the war had been going on almost since the world had begun. It seemed incredible to think that it might end.

Räv brushed a silvery lock from her forehead. "That's why I've been waiting here for you all this time. Vatten's enemies might not trust a message sent to them directly by his former followers, but as the Guardian, you're supposed to be neutral, which makes you the perfect go-between. The rebels sent me here to ask you to arrange a meeting between us and our former opponents."

Mr. Hu's mustache twitched. "Why should I believe you? You have deceived me and my apprentice every time we've met."

Räv scratched the back of her head. "I was afraid you'd

bring up that minor detail."

The boy's temper flared. "I wouldn't call those things minor. You almost got us killed."

"I'm telling the truth for once," Räv protested.

"It would be good news," Mr. Hu said warily, "if Vatten were to lose strength here."

Räv spread her arms as if she were trying to embrace a globe. "It's not just in San Francisco. When Vatten couldn't find the Guardians in China, he began sending the Clan of the Nine all around the world, including here. There's been rebellion everywhere he sent us."

Mr. Hu lifted his head sharply. "Just how many rebels are there?"

"Lots," Räv boasted. "Enough to give you a chance to beat Vatten if we can combine forces."

"Why are you here alone?" Mr. Hu asked, glancing around. "Why aren't there more of the rebels with you?"

"San Francisco's flooded with the Clan of the Nine still loyal to Vatten," she said, glancing around cautiously. "They want to put down the revolt, so the other rebels here have gone into hiding. They're just waiting for word from me about the meeting."

Mistral leaned forward, narrowing her eyes suspiciously. "How do we know this is not some sort of trick?"

Most people would have begun trembling if a dragon—even a disguised one—gazed at them that way, but Räv said coolly, "You can wait until Vatten destroys the world. Or you can listen to me." She faced the Guardian again. "But we anticipated your mistrust, and so we are prepared to offer hostages and other securities if the others will do the same while we meet."

Sidney squinted at her suspiciously as he circled her. "Watch out, Mr. H. My mother always said that if a deal sounds too good to be true, then it probably is."

"And yet if we could end this terrible war," Mr. Hu murmured as if he were tempted, "it would be a step toward creating a lasting peace." He gave a thoughtful nod. "I'll see if any of my acquaintances will even come. I think my home is best because it's neutral territory."

"Just a moment," Mistral snapped. "You said you only found out about the rebellion in the Clan when you went home. So why were you following us before that?"

The girl hesitated. "Maybe I was curious."

"I would have avoided us at all cost." The dragon glowered. "She's hiding something, Hu. This proves she's planning to steal the egg for herself."

"I don't have to tell you my reasons," she said with a flip of her head. "The Clan of the Nine came not only to put down the rebellion but to find you. Without me, Vatten would have had scouts here, but I put so many false clues around the city that they're running up one hill and down another."

"That's easy to claim, but what proof do you have?" Mistral demanded.

Räv bristled defiantly. "None. But without me, you'll never reach home—I'm the only one who can show you the safe route."

"I say we eliminate her once and for all," Mistral argued as she crouched. "I'll handle it if you're too squeamish, Hu."

However deceitful she might be, no one could deny Räv's courage as she bravely squared her shoulders. "I was a fool to think you'd believe me. Go on! Throw away your best hope for peace!"

If she was lying, Tom thought, she must be the greatest actor in the world, and he couldn't help thinking of another fool. Ring Neck had been a coward for so many years, and yet in the end, he had been the bravest one of them. For whatever her reasons, perhaps Räv was trying to be honest now. "Everyone can change, I guess."

Mr. Hu regarded his apprentice. "So you believe her?"

Once again the Guardian was seeking his opinion. "I . . . I think she's telling the truth," Tom mumbled. He just hoped he wasn't guessing wrong.

Mr. Hu's chin sunk to his chest and then he raised his head again. "So be it."

Räv said almost wistfully, "Tom doesn't know how lucky he is to have you as his master."

"I'll be keeping my eye on you," the hostile dragon warned, "and at the first sign of treachery. . . ." She drew a finger across her throat.

Monkey stared first in one direction and then the other down the empty street.

"We'll be here forever if we wait for a taxi," Monkey said. "We'll have to walk."

There was nothing for them to do but trudge through the dimly lit streets and over a steep hill to reach China-town by a route that Räv assured them was safe.

The streetlamps shone like pale will-o'-the wisps, and soon they came to the foot of a hill. Even though the slope angled up sharply, Tom felt new energy now that he was on land again. He saw that the others were walking briskly too as Räv led them with the suspicious dragon close on her heels, ready to punish the girl at a moment's notice.

Checking over her shoulder, Räv stared at Tom. "Why did you streak your hair and start wearing yellow con-tacts?"

Mr. Hu gave a slight shake of his head, so Tom tried to pass it off as a joke. "Do you like my new look?"

Räv appeared doubtful, but she folded her arms and asked, "What happened in the park anyway? They carried you out of that hill and back to Chinatown. And the next thing I knew, you came practically bouncing out of the store while Mr. Hu looked so weak."

"You were following us even then?" Tom asked in sur-prise.

"You had me worried. I waited around the museum for a while, but when you didn't come out, I went home."

"I don't think you need to know anymore than that," Mr. Hu said with a warning glance at his apprentice.

"We're allies now," she coaxed. "You still don't trust me?"

"First, demonstrate that we can," Mr. Hu said firmly.

"I will—if it kills me," she said, striding on with a stiffened back, even more determined than before.

Mistral was the only one who cast glances behind her toward the bay. After all her years of exile, Tom knew what the sea had meant to her. "Do you miss your home already?" Tom asked.

Mistral shook her head. "Not the home, but that idiot. Once a fool always a fool, I suppose." And she lapsed into a brooding silence as she kept her eyes upon Räv's back.

Suddenly they heard a clinking sound like someone tapping a giant pot, but there was no one to be seen on the street. From somewhere farther away, someone else clinked in answer.

Mr. Hu raised a hand to stop them, his nostrils widening as he tested the air suspiciously. "Something's not right."

"There shouldn't be Clan here," Räv said, nervously peering about.

"If you're up to your old tricks, you'll pay," Mistral growled, wrapping her fingers around the girl's throat.

Stepping up beside his master, Tom inhaled sharply. San Francisco did not get many lightning storms, but Tom remembered at least one time when he had smelled the ozone. He caught a faint whiff of something like that now.

Mr. Hu opened his large tiger eyes as he took in great gusts of the damp air. "There's magic somewhere."

"Want me to fly and scout around, Mr. H.?" Sidney volunteered.

The streetlamp ahead of them sputtered and went out. One by one, the other lights went dark until there was only the faint light from the moon.

"Where are they?" Mr. Hu turned in a slow circle. "I smell them, but I don't see them."

Suddenly there was a loud clang. Tom spun around to see that a nearby manhole cover had been thrown onto the wet street behind them, and out of the hole scrambled the oddest bunch of men and women. With the help of the moon, he could just make out their black fur coats and top hats. Their faces were all blue and each seemed to be clutching a tube in his or her mouth.

The revelation spell was the one bit of magic Tom had mastered long ago and he muttered it now so that their true forms were revealed. They crouched, faces still blue, but their coats had turned to dark, glossy pelts and the hats into tall tufts of hair gathered like sheaves of black wheat. And their mouths had become narrow muzzles.

One of them threw back his head and let out a long ululation.

"The *yen huo*," Monkey said, taking out his staff as the furry black monsters swarmed onto the street.

"So you did lead us into an ambush!" Mistral said, tightening her grip on Räv's throat.

Räv made choking sounds as she tried to pull the fingers away. "I swear I . . . thought this way . . . was all right."

From up ahead they heard answering cries, and Tom could see shadowy shapes in front of them.

As Mistral's fingers tightened, Räv held out her hands desperately to the Guardian. "I didn't . . . lead you into an ambush . . . honest."

"We'll settle with you later," Mr. Hu growled as the yen huo closed on them.

"You . . . don't believe me?" Räv's shoulders sagged and her arms dropped.

"We don't have time for revenge now." He patted Mistral's paw. "Master Thomas, keep her prisoner until we can deal with her later."

As the girl was passed to him, she pleaded with Tom. "It was the truth!"

Tom gripped her arm tightly. "Save it," he said suspiciously, and gazed at the dark creatures coming toward them.

The yen huo were the size of adult humans; Tom saw no fangs or claws. Though there were about two dozen of them scurrying on all fours, Mistral combined with Mr. Hu and Monkey seemed far deadlier as they took their true shapes.

As the lead yen huo opened his mouth as if to shout again, Sidney folded his arms. "What's so scary about them?"

"That!" Mr. Hu yanked Tom, the girl, and the rat down so hard that they plopped onto the sidewalk. A jet of flame shot from the mouth of the yen huo. Tom could smell a stink like a backed-up sewer.

No sooner did the first yen huo close his mouth than another spewed fire. "They'd be popular at barbecues," Monkey said as he squatted. "I wish we had some of that dream dust left."

"I think I got a fire extinguisher in here somewhere," Sidney said, patting his fur. "But it's only a small one."

"Then save it for the flammable," Mistral said. Like a black lightning bolt, she launched herself at the yen huo. Their flames bounced off her leathery hide as she knocked them left and right.

Sidney was already scampering in her wake as the tiger hauled Tom and Räv to their feet. "After her."

With Monkey bringing up the rear, they raced past the stunned yen huo, who lay sprawled on either side. Mr. Hu's paws swatted aside the few that Mistral had missed.

When they reached the next street, they heard a rumbling, as if huge motorcycles were ahead of them. The next moment, half a dozen men loped around the corner and into the intersection.

Their long, unkempt hair hung over their ears and

down their shoulders and their bodies were long and lean; they bounded down the asphalt on pipe-stem arms and legs. The thunderous sound was coming from their throats.

This time Mr. Hu cast the revelation spell, stripping away their disguise. Their heads stayed more or less human except for the protruding ox ears, and each now had a solitary eye in the center of his face. Their bodies became sleek as leopards with long tails and they roared defiantly.

"*Chu chien*," Mr. Hu said, flattening his ears as he crouched.

A car crossing the intersection bought them a little time as it screeched to a halt. The driver began to honk his horn angrily until he got a better look at the chu chien. One of them bounded onto his car and thumping its bony tail on the hood let out a horrific roar, showing Tom its sharp fangs. They would not be as easy as the yen huo.

"Kamsin, Kamsin!" Mistral shouted, eager for battle as she lashed her tail.

Räv was so desperate to prove she had told them the truth that she wrenched free from Tom's grip. "I'll show you that they hate me as much as they do you," she said as she pulled a stiletto from a sheath hidden by her sleeve.

Tom's hands froze in midreach to grab her. "What are you going to do?"

"This." And Räv charged toward Vatten's monsters.

Immediately a chu chien swung away from the dragon and surged forward, baring its fangs at the girl. Räv nimbly escaped its lunge, dodging, skipping, and wriggling as she avoided one deadly blow after another.

Monkey narrowed his eyes. "They could be under orders to fake an attack."

A paw sent Räv sprawling.

"That blood on her arm isn't fake." Tom started forward as the chu chien reared up to slash her.

Monkey was quicker. Somersaulting along the street, he straddled the girl. His ringed staff seemed to be everywhere, striking a head here and a paw there, as much a part of him as his tail. When he had driven the monsters back, he gathered her up and brought her to Mr. Hu and the others.

"I think they broke a rib." Räv winced as Monkey laid her down on the sidewalk and she felt her side. "No, I guess it's only bruised."

"That was a fool thing to do," Mr. Hu said, kneeling beside her. With a bandage from Sidney's stores, he gently covered the slash on her arm.

"It was the only way to convince you," she panted in pain. She looked up earnestly. "Have I?"

Mr. Hu was genuinely puzzled. "Why is my opinion so important that you'd risk your life for it?"

Tom didn't find it so puzzling. She had spoken so admiringly of the Guardian, saying the boy was lucky to have such a master. "Is that the real reason you've been following us?"

Räv's cheeks reddened as she struggled to her feet, favoring her injured side. "I told you it was curiosity. I've never met anyone like Mr. Hu before."

Sidney nudged the tiger. "You've got a girlfriend, Mr. H."

"Be quiet, you fool rat," Mr. Hu scolded, then said to the girl, "you've certainly proved your courage if not your good sense."

Monkey swung his staff around, ready to join Mistral, but Mr. Hu held him back. "We don't have time for a battle. The Clan of the Nine will be coming here from all over the city now that they know we're back in town."

"Can you summon the rebels?" Mr. Hu asked her.

Räv shook her head. "They wouldn't get here in time."

Monkey looked at their enemies in dismay. "What do we do, Hu? Neither you nor the children can fly like Sidney."

Tom had been looking all around them. They were standing right in front of an apartment house that, like so many buildings in San Francisco, was crammed right next to its neighbor. Since there was no room on the sides, the fire escape was on the front.

"No," the boy said and pointed at it, "but we can climb."

CHAPTER THIRTEEN

⤜✦⤛

The jen-mien hsiao has a body like a monkey and a tail like a dog.
Its head is shaped like an owl's, but with a human face.

—Shan Hai Ching

The p'ao hsiao has a goat's body, but with a human face and nails
and a tiger's fangs. Its eyes are behind its front legs.

—Shan Hai Ching

Mr. Hu nodded when he saw what Tom was pointing at. "Sidney."

"Right on it, Mr. H.," Sidney said. His fur began to shimmer and the rat expanded as if he were a balloon until his outline started to blur with a loud humming sound, then he lurched into the air like a fuzzy helicopter. Seizing the bottom rung of the fire escape, the rat yanked it down with a loud rattle and thud. Tom let Räv go up first and then climbed after her to the first story of the building.

With all of his old energy, Mr. Hu sprang easily onto the third rung and followed them quickly.

Below them, they saw Mistral in the midst of the chu chien, tail swinging, claws sweeping, fangs flashing, heedless of the wounds she might take as long as she could beat her enemies. Monkey flew overhead, striking with his staff, but the flames were flashing nearer and nearer.

"The yen huo have almost caught up with us," he said to Mistral. "You don't have time to spread your wings before they'll be on top of you. Better take the stairs. I'll hold them off."

But the dragon stepped farther away. "I'll buy you time."

"Hurry up!" Sidney shouted. "The rest of Vatten's monsters will be closing in."

"Let them." Mistral laughed. Her tail thumped several chu chien against a building. Throwing back her head, she shouted, "Kamsin, Kamsin!" Her battle cry echoed defiantly against the quiet buildings.

"She'll get herself killed," Tom said anxiously.

"I think she wants to die," Mr. Hu said grimly.

"I don't understand," Tom said, feeling helpless.

Mr. Hu put a foreleg around Tom's shoulders. "I don't pretend to understand affairs of the heart, but I believe that without Ring Neck, she's lost the will to live."

"She wants to quit?" Tom asked.

Sidney put it more succinctly. "Her heart's broken, poor kid."

Fighting tears, Tom started back down as he shouted, "Mistral, come with us!" He remembered how grief-stricken he was when he thought she was lost in the volcano. He repeated what they had said at the land gate. "You'll only make the king happy if you get yourself killed."

This time it didn't work. "I have to die some time. I

189

always knew it would be in a battle," Mistral said, the despair plain in her voice now. He had seen how determined she could be when she wanted to live; but hearing her now, Tom knew the Guardian was right. Now all she wanted to do was join Ring Neck in death.

Tom hesitated, knowing he should escape to the roof but reluctant to desert his friend. "I'm sorry about Ring Neck, but you're not alone. We're your friends." He glanced behind him at the Guardian for support.

More accustomed to dealing with spells than people's feelings, the tiger adjusted his tie. "Yes, exactly what Master Thomas said." When Tom cleared his throat noisily, Mr. Hu scratched his head uncomfortably. "In fact, we're more than that," he added. "We're . . . um . . ." The Guardian looked helplessly at the boy, for once at a loss for words.

"We're family," Tom suggested.

"Yes, just so," Mr. Hu called. "You'll always have a place with us."

When Mistral sagged with a groan, Tom was afraid at first that she had suffered a wound. "That isn't fair," she said.

Monkey hovered overhead, sweeping his staff in great arcs—the yen huo kept a respectful distance, but they were edging closer, shooting out darts of flame that singed the ape's robe. "Can we carry on this chat somewhere else?" he panted.

"Humph," Mistral grumbled, "if you and Hu want to

persist in this delusion, I'll humor you." She cast a baleful eye up toward the ape. "But I refuse to accept any kind of relationship to this furbag."

The tiger pivoted, winking at Tom as if to say *well done*. "Up the fire escape you go, Master Thomas, and make room for our 'cousin.'"

Tom began to climb, looking over his shoulder to make sure his friend was slithering up after Mr. Hu. Sidney disappeared above him as Tom ascended, but the steps, damp from the evening air, were slippery and he could not move as fast as he would have liked. He could feel Mr. Hu close behind him.

"It looks all clear on the roof," Sidney called down. "I've got Räv with me."

Mistral drew the bottom set of steps up and smashed the mechanism. Beneath her the Clan snarled and leaped, trying to reach them. Tom stood close beside the ladder and saw that Mistral was limping when she stepped onto the roof. "You're hurt."

"Not as badly as that scum that attacked us," the dragon said with bitter satisfaction.

As she joined them on the rooftop, Mr. Hu frowned and pointed to a bank of fog rolling speedily toward them like a huge wave of cotton. "That's no summer mist."

Tom could feel the back of his neck tingle slightly. "It's magical."

"Who knows what monsters it's hiding?" Sidney shivered.

"But what may conceal our enemies may also conceal us from them," Mr. Hu noted grimly. "There is no need for secrecy now, only speed. It's time to take to the air." He cleared his throat. "I wouldn't normally ask this, Mistral, but times are desperate. Will you take Master Thomas, Räv, and myself?"

"I have no dignity left." Mistral sighed. "And anyway, you're my kin now." She crouched and unfurled her wings. "Get on if you want a ride. But don't get used to it."

Tom hauled himself up on her back just behind her neck. Her scales were burned and dented and even broken in places. He wanted to pet her, but he felt instinctively that the dragon would be insulted. Räv scrambled up nimbly behind him.

Mr. Hu leaped up beside her. "Hang on tight, Master Thomas."

Tom pressed himself flat against the dragon's back and gripped between the dents. Monkey and Sidney were already hovering overhead. With a mighty spring and flap of her wings, Mistral rose into the air to join them.

His first ride on a dragon might have been exciting if he could have seen something, but Tom barely had time to glance at the street below when the fog rolled over them— and then there was only mist and more mist.

"So which way, Hu?" Mistral asked.

Mr. Hu hesitated and then pointed. "We have to head southeast."

They flew slowly due to the mist over the silent city, and Tom sat up. Above them the moon was only a glowing, ill-defined spot, and below them the streetlamps were just as indistinct. Sidney was flying on ahead and they heard a muffled cry.

"Are you all right?" Mr. Hu called.

"Yeah," Sidney answered, "but there's a tall apartment building ahead. I just found it the hard way. I think my muzzle's bent."

Sidney descended a moment later. "We went too far. We're in the Mission, but I think I know where we are."

They had gone only about a hundred yards when Sidney shouted, "Watch out!"

Screeching little men and women suddenly plunged out of the fog. As Mr. Hu raised a paw he growled to his apprentice, "Master Thomas, if you please, would you show us what we're fighting?"

Tom almost wished he hadn't lifted the enchantment when he saw what nightmares they were. Their furry bodies were closest to apes and their paws had opposable thumbs with which they grasped machetes, but their short tails didn't seem as flexible. Their heads were feathery globes like owls, but instead of beaks they had human noses, eyes, and mouths.

Mistral swatted away a pair with her right paw.

"*Jen-mien hsiao*," the dragon said, as if it were a curse word.

Monkey was swinging his staff, but more of them darted at the desperate travelers. Mr. Hu pressed Tom and Räv flat against Mistral's back. Small determined paws tugged at him as the jen-mien tried to pull him off. With a growl, the Guardian swept a paw that sent them tumbling away.

Beneath him, Tom felt the dragon's powerful muscles as she tried to fly and fight at the same time. Mistral had to writhe and wriggle through the air, sometimes halting with a jerk as she flapped her wings, trying to shake off the jen-mien. Though they had no claws and their teeth were too small to damage the dragon's hide, they tried to cling to her wings and by sheer weight of numbers force her down. Monkey was kept busy darting from side to side, clearing them away with his staff from the dragon until they had been driven off.

Then Tom remembered their other friend. "Sidney," he called into the mist. "Are you all right?"

All he heard, though, was the screeching of the strange winged creatures pursuing them.

"I'm afraid we're going to end up like the rat," Mistral panted. "There are too many of them."

"They're trying to drive us down to the street," Mr. Hu said. "Keep going."

Tom clung sadly to the dragon, trying to stay on. First his grandmother, then Ring Neck, and now Sidney.

Who was going to be next?

Suddenly, to his great surprise, he heard the rat yell, "This way, Mr. H!"

"He's still alive," Tom gasped.

"He's indestructible," Mr. Hu said, chuckling in relief.

The rat suddenly popped up in front of Tom like some giant bumblebee. His fur was torn in places and he was clutching one paw, but he winked at the boy. "These parakeets are nothing compared to the pigeons in Union Square." He slid in front of Tom so he could sit on the dragon's back. "But I could use a rest."

Mistral and Monkey changed direction slightly at Sidney's instruction, heading down when he told them. They passed over one rooftop after another, skimming over old rusty television antennas that stood up like bare metal trees.

Then the boy began to feel as if ants were crawling under his skin again. "I feel some strong *ch'i*."

Mr. Hu gave a great sniff. "It's coming up. Yes, land here."

"How can you tell? It looks just like the others," Mistral said skeptically, but she landed anyway.

"A long time ago, someone used to dry fish on the roof of the building next to mine," Mr. Hu said, hopping off. "There are traces of it if you have a sensitive enough nose. Right, Master Thomas?"

"Yes," Tom said, covering his nose because he too could smell the faint odor of dead, drying fish. There were some disadvantages to sharing tiger's blood.

The fog had cleared enough on the roof for Tom to see a small shack that housed a rusty metal door. The tiger bounded toward it on all fours, scattering gravel across the roof in all directions. Mistral and Monkey glanced all around. "They've gone."

"Maybe they're scared of Mr. Hu's wards," Tom said as he slid from the dragon's back.

"Wards would keep them out once we were inside but wouldn't drive them away," Mistral said, still studying the fog.

"I'm just glad to be rid of them," Sidney said as Tom helped him off.

Suddenly they heard a wail from behind the shack.

"I think our playmates decided to leave us to a new batch," Monkey said, getting ready with his staff.

The next moment fifty men trotted from around the shack on all fours. Their hair had been knotted into long ponytails on either side of their heads and they were bare waisted despite the chill, damp air. Their heads remained stiff on their necks like mannequins as they swung their chests to face the group.

When Tom muttered the revelation spell, the ponytails became horns and the intruders stood exposed as goats about the size of Mr. Hu—but with human heads that were now eyeless.

It was only when the goats had placed themselves

squarely in front of the door to safety that Tom saw the red eyes blinking at him. They were on the body behind the front legs, so that the goats had to stand slightly sideways to look at them.

"What's that?" Tom gulped.

"A *p'ao hsiao*," Monkey said as he headed to help his friend.

The Guardian crouched, flattening his ears angrily. "Step aside if you value your life."

One of the p'aos exposed fangs as deadly as the tiger's. "Do you think we fear you more than Lord Vatten?" Throwing back his head, he gave a new cry.

From out of the fog they heard another p'ao's mournful acknowledgment, then another and another, from all over Chinatown, as if a horde of ghosts were sweeping toward them.

CHAPTER FOURTEEN

"We'll take care of them, Hu. Just get that door open," Monkey said as he sprang forward, staff raised over his head. "Once we're inside, your wards should keep us safe, but out in the open on the roof we're easy targets."

"You don't have time to fight all of them before reinforcements arrive." Räv nodded urgently toward the tiger's pocket. "Release the hsieh from the rock. They'll drive away your enemies so you can get inside."

Mr. Hu hesitated as the howling drew ever closer. "The hsieh belong to the Clan of the Nine, just like those things. Even if you have turned away from Vatten, it would be folly to let *them* loose."

A note of anger crept into the girl's voice. "I understand their speech. They were cursing Vatten when they were left to die. They'll follow him no more—hey!" she cried, cringing when the tiger leaned forward and sniffed her.

He straightened. "I don't smell fear. I think you believe what you're saying."

Tom stared at Räv uncertainly and then tested the air discreetly with his own nose. "I don't think she's lying either; but if she's wrong . . ."

"Prudence dictates we leave." Mr. Hu growled.

As Tom saw their enemies crouching in anticipation of an attack, his tiger's blood began racing through him until it was almost a kind of electricity filling him with energy. From the way that Mr. Hu's tail was lashing, Tom knew he was feeling the same thing.

"But what does your blood tell you?" Tom asked.

The tiger grinned. "It says to take the gamble."

"Hu!" Mistral gasped. "Think of the stakes!"

"There have been cautious Guardians and there have been Guardians who loved risk," Mr. Hu said as he fished the green rock from his pocket. "Prudence dictated remaining in China even in the midst of all the chaos, but the Guardian at that time decided to come to America and there was relative peace for him and his successors until now."

Despite his bold words, the tiger first insisted on some precautions, mounting with Tom upon Mistral's back so they could take off if the hsieh turned on them instead. Räv, though, insisted she had to be with them when they were released.

"They may not trust me otherwise," she explained.

"I think something's coming," Monkey said, squinting. "But I can't tell how far away." He pointed at shadowy smudges in the mist.

"They're flying." Sidney slipped his hatchet from his fur. "Once they're here, we may not be able to escape by air."

"Think again, Hu," Mistral begged as she spread her wings.

However, Mr. Hu was already breathing upon the green rock and mumbling a spell, and then he tossed it into the air. Immediately, the ball began to crumble like dry, brittle clay, releasing what looked like a blue-and-red mist. The mist, though, swelled into mottled dots that settled on the rooftop.

As Tom watched, the points expanded until he could see the red-scaled dogs with coarse blue hair bristling along their spines and skulls. They let out happy yips and gurgles as they wheeled about, surprised to be in the open air again and greeting one another.

Räv waded into their middle, laughing as the hsieh rose on hind legs to lick at her face. When she was in the center, she raised her hands to calm them. "The Guardian has freed you, and even better he offers you revenge." She pointed toward the p'aos with her stiletto. "If we drive them away, we hurt Vatten—the one who left us to die so horribly." She raised her hands. "Will you come with me?"

A hound reared its head and answered her with a long,

angry wail. And then another and another.

Drawing the stiletto from her sleeve, she whirled around. Her eyes were almost as wild as when Mr. Hu became pure tiger. "I'll show you how much the hsieh hate Vatten," she declared to the Guardian.

The tiger called down to her, worried. "All I ask is that you distract them long enough for us to get inside."

With a strange smile, she stroked the heads of the nearest hsieh. "Vatten counted us for little. We'll show him how wrong he was." Spreading her arms, she cried to the hsieh. "Come! Let's drive this scum away!"

She began running toward the p'aos again, not even bothering to see if the hsieh were following her.

The blue-and-scarlet hounds poured after her.

"She's mad," Mistral murmured.

"She's got nothing to lose," Tom said, thinking of Mistral's own reckless courage.

"And everything to win," Monkey said. "She wants Hu to like her."

"The poor child," the tiger said, shaking his head. "What kind of life has she led where my feeble friendship counts more than her life?"

Räv and the hounds struck the p'aos like an avalanche, driving them to either side except for a thin line just before the shack. Then the p'aos rallied and surged back, and for a moment the rooftop was filled with dozens of small, swirling battles.

Tom watched breathlessly as the girl held her own in the center of the p'aos, her blade rising and falling.

"We can't leave all the fun to her," Monkey said, nudging Mistral.

For once the dragon agreed with the ape. "No, of course not." She glanced over her shoulder. "Right, Hu?"

"Right," Mr. Hu snarled, and springing down to the rooftop, helped Tom slide off the dragon's back.

Despite her wounds and fatigue, the dragon's legs tensed like huge coils and hurled her forward like a glittering, scaled spear. Monkey bounded into the air after her, twirling his staff like a propeller.

As soon as Monkey and Mistral started forward, the Guardian motioned to Tom and Sidney. "Stick close to me."

Their attack caught Vatten's creatures by surprise. Monkey swung his staff like a terrible whirlwind, striking down any who might chance his way. Mistral did not even bother with her fangs or claws but became an armored battering ram.

Then, like the perfect fighting machine he was, the tiger leaped upon their enemies. The slender but muscular legs carried the powerful body with a lithe grace, and his slashing fangs and claws made him seem like a dancer wielding knives in some deadly ballet. Tom thought he had never seen anyone as beautiful or as frightening.

The tiger gave a roar from deep in his throat, like a

giant file rasping against a rusty blade. His challenge carried across the Chinatown roofs louder and clearer than any trumpet.

As the echo rang in his ears, Tom felt his heart pound faster and faster; and the energy inside him swelled and crackled like a lightning storm. Throwing back his head, the boy roared in answer to his master and struck out with his fists. In his fury, there was no time to think about spells.

With frightened wails, the p'aos began to leave in twos and threes, and then it was a wholesale rout as they escaped into the fog.

"Well done!" Räv shouted to the hsieh, who leaped on her and one another in celebration. She faced Mr. Hu as he came to her. "And what are your orders now?"

Mr. Hu's sides heaving underneath his vest and coat, he panted, "I am not their master."

Even so, the hsieh watched him, tongues panting.

"You're free," Mr. Hu insisted.

"They'll work mischief for someone," Mistral cautioned.

"But not near us," Mr. Hu said, and leaned forward. "Do you hear me? Stay out of Chinatown, out of San Francisco, out of the country."

Räv slipped the stiletto into the sheath hidden inside her sleeve. "Do you hear him? Go far away. Enjoy yourselves."

Even so, the hsieh still hesitated until Mr. Hu clapped his paws together. "Yes, go."

A hound threw back his head and let out a triumphant wail, and the pack surged over the rooftops like a red-and-blue tide, yipping and wailing as they disappeared into the mist.

CHAPTER FiFTEEN

Master Yen
There once was a wizard who created robots so lifelike that people
thought they were alive. He used leather, wood, gum, lacquer, and
the magical colors of white, black, red, and blue.

—The Lieh Tzu

Ch'ih Yu
When a mountain split open in an earthquake, he was the first to
take the ore he found and make metal weapons. His head was of
bronze and his brow of iron, and he dined on stone pebbles.

—Shu Ching

"Hurry, Hu," Monkey urged. In the distance they heard an ominous thudding—as if from heavy paws. And a giant shadowy shape had appeared in the opposite direction from the one the hounds had taken.

"One of the p'aos' reinforcements, no doubt," Mr. Hu said. He took out a large ring of keys and unlocked the roof door but didn't open it right away. Instead, he placed a paw upon the rusty surface and began to murmur, careful to keep his back to Räv while he muttered a spell to open it.

The creature loomed ever larger, and they heard pieces of the other buildings crumbling under the monster's weight and falling to the street.

"Whatever's coming looks awfully big. What are you waiting for?" Räv asked anxiously.

"He's deactivating the ward that's there," Tom explained, feeling just as antsy as the girl. One of the monsters looked as large as the Dragon King. "Don't distract him."

The group was silent, one eye upon the Guardian and one eye upon the shape. Screeches began to echo across Chinatown, and red eyes began to glow like burning coals in the grayness. It was still hard to make out their exact outline, but Tom thought he saw thick, curved talons.

Suddenly Mr. Hu yanked open the door with a loud creak of rusty hinges, and Tom, who had never been above the ground floor of the building, saw that the door was made of several inches of solid steel.

Sidney let out a whistle. "That looks like it came from Fort Knox!"

"My uncle wasn't one to take chances." Mr. Hu gave him an exhausted smile and then nodded at the rat. "Sidney, loan your flashlight to Master Thomas, will you?"

"I hope the batteries work," Sidney said as he took it from his fur and handed it to Tom.

Tom was glad he had the light when he went down the steps. The daylight from the doorway was lost in the dusty attic. By the flashlight beam, he saw vases, wardrobes, furniture, and piles of boxes all jumbled together.

"Get inside!" Mr. Hu yelled. He shoved Räv and she

fell down the stairs, knocking the boy off his feet, and they fell, tumbling together, onto the dusty floor.

"Jeepers, jeepers," a frightened Sidney was muttering as his claws scrabbled down the steps.

"Oof," Mistral grunted. "Why did your uncle have to scrimp on the doorways?"

"You refugee from a handbag factory, you're still duchess size!" Monkey snapped from the rooftop. They heard his staff clang when it struck at their pursuers, who let out horrifying howls. "I thought your pride would get you killed one day, but did you have to do that to your friends as well?"

"Hurry up and shrink," Mr. Hu said, and then he was roaring out his battle cry as he joined the fight.

Tom looked up the stairs past Sidney. The bright rectangle of the doorway was blocked partly by Mistral's shoulders, but her long head was inside.

"We've got to help her," Tom said as he struggled to his feet.

The next moment, though, Mistral had shrunk so she could slither inside. Monkey clambered over her back before she was halfway through, and to Tom's relief, Mr. Hu came last, almost treading on her tail.

Purple talons, each as thick as Tom's arm, raked the empty air, and a monster screeched in frustration.

Mr. Hu spun around. "Help me close the door," he grunted as he strained to pull it shut.

Mistral's long neck arched past them, snapping at whatever was holding the door open. While she defended them with her fangs, the tiger and ape managed to slam it shut.

Instantly it was as pitch-black as the depths of the sea, and Tom swung the flashlight to illuminate the door where Mr. Hu stood muttering a spell while Monkey fought to keep it shut. Finally the tiger breathed a sigh of relief and turned, his eyes glowing like amber jewels. "It's done."

He was the only one who did not jump when something thudded against the door, trying to batter it down. And he was the only one who remained still when the door crackled and sizzled, and the monster screeched in pain from the contact.

"Master Thomas," Mr. Hu asked, adjusting his cuffs, "would you be so kind as to move forward to make room for the rest of our guests?" The tiger's paws made shooing motions as he herded Monkey and Mistral down the steps.

Keeping the flashlight trained behind him so the others could see, Tom shuffled down the narrow aisle, but it meandered between so many objects that he kept bumping into things. Though the tiger could see quite well in the dark, his guests did not, so that there were bruised shins and paws before they reached the rickety stairs and descended into the apartment itself.

The thumping on the roof indicated that they had more company, and though they could see nothing through the window of the store in front of the apartment, they saw shadowy creatures prowling in the alley outside. They were under siege.

Mistral glanced uneasily at the front door. "Hu, will your wards hold against a massive assault?"

"Are you doubting my magic?" Mr. Hu asked indignantly.

"No, but they do seem to have the numbers," Monkey said.

Tom remembered how Vatten's monsters had overwhelmed his grandmother's own wards.

"Help is only a phone call away," Räv boasted as she helped herself to a cookie. "Lady Torka is one of the leaders of the rebels, and she's in the city."

"I know her by reputation. She's a deadly fighter." Mr. Hu arched his eyebrows politely. "But are you sure she'll talk to you?"

Räv strolled confidently to the telephone. "She says the rebellion can't happen without me. If I give her the word, she'll bring all our people with her. And she'll even summon the rest of the rebels from all around the world to help you protect the phoenix."

"Then I shall do my part." As he sat down, Mr. Hu motioned toward the desk. "Master Thomas, fetch me some paper and my writing things. Oh, and don't forget the matches and the ashtray."

As Tom got the items, Räv attempted to use the telephone but then slammed down the receiver in disgust. "They've cut the lines. I should've expected that."

"I would have done no less if I were them," Mr. Hu said as he began to write a letter in a strange script.

Suddenly the streetlights went out one by one with loud pops, and it was black as Chinese ink outside.

As Monkey readied his staff and Mistral heaved herself from the floor, a subdued Räv chewed her lip. She'd obviously been counting on her fellow rebels saving them. "Vatten's monsters are getting ready to attack."

"Let them," Mr. Hu said as he lit his missive. Tom was used to the Guardian's postal system, but Räv gawked.

Before she could ask, Tom informed her with a grin, "Mr. Hu's sending out letters."

He grabbed a quick meal of cookies while Mr. Hu wrote and posted more letters. It was only when he declared himself done that the tiger sipped some lukewarm tea and munched cookies.

The replies began to materialize from the air before the Guardian could brush away all the crumbs from his vest, and Tom was kept busy catching them while the Guardian began to read. When the boy heard the rumbling sound like an idling pickup truck, he knew it must be good news because that was the sound of the tiger's purr.

"The Dark Lady will come from China as soon as

she can," Mr. Hu announced.

Mistral had been keeping an anxious watch on the dark alley. "She'd better not take too long. We'll need her strategy." She glanced at Monkey, who was still eating. "You haven't stolen something from her, have you?"

"No," the ape said thoughtfully, as if mulling over future possibilities.

"Who is she?" Tom asked.

Mr. Hu smiled. "You won't find a statue of her in Chinatown, if that's what you mean." He waved a paw toward Grant Avenue. "And that's true of most of the heroes whom I'm inviting to the meeting. They performed their deeds in the days when the world was first born— before books and writing and even farming were discovered so most of their deeds have been forgotten over the millennia. And yet without them, the world would have been destroyed on several different occasions."

"That's not fair," Tom protested.

Mr. Hu shrugged. "The statues you see in Chinatown and the stories you've learned about them belong to the younger lords and ladies." He laid one paw over the other. "But China has been piling legends and heroes on top of one another for more than four thousand years. Statues get made only for those from the most recent layer. The statues of our guests are buried in the rubble of vanished cities, and even when they're dug up, the features are so worn that archaeologists can't tell who they are. So if our guests are sensitive to slights, you'll understand why."

Tom thought about his parents, who had disappeared on an archaeological dig. "Was that what my parents were doing?"

Mr. Hu scratched the tip of his muzzle. "Yes, I believe Master Paul's interest was prehistory."

The group gave a jump when something banged against the front window, trying to break the glass. A moment later, they heard more sizzlings and cracklings and a pained howl.

Mr. Hu paid no attention to the attacker but looked through another letter instead. "And K'ua Fu still has his doubts, but he's willing to accept a temporary truce. He'll also be here as fast as he can travel."

Monkey clapped a paw over his eyes. "Uh, whenever he gets excited, he gives me a headache."

"I thought nothing bothered you," Tom said.

"I just hope that doesn't happen, but if it does"— Monkey turned to Sidney—"I may need some aspirin from you."

The rat began to rummage around in his fur. "Let's see. I got that family-size bottle in here somewhere."

"Can you send a letter for me?" Räv asked, with a worried glance at the darkness beyond the store.

Mr. Hu brushed his whiskers. "You'll need to describe the person to me."

"Well, the Lady Torka looks like a fox but with the

loveliest red fur." Räv motioned to her shoulders. "And she has a pair of wings."

"What's their span when they're spread out?" Mr. Hu asked intently.

He asked questions about the minutest details until even Tom thought he could picture Lady Torka in his own mind.

When Räv had written the letter for help, Mr. Hu burned it for her and then resumed his reading. The most ornate letter, of course, came from the king of the dragons.

Mr. Hu tore open the envelope, and his amber eyes darted down the columns of words on the gilt paper. "He has reservations about an alliance, but he's willing to listen."

"Any apology?" Tom asked.

Mr. Hu laughed. "Of course not. The dragons were born almost at the creation of the world and deep is their knowledge, but they have yet to learn the meaning of the word 'sorry.'"

Sidney nudged Mr. Hu's kneecap. "Um, Mr. H., let me know if he mentions some missing silverware or towels, will you?"

The tiger frowned at the rat. "What makes you think His Highness would concern himself with your petty thievery?"

"They were souvenirs," a wounded Sidney defended himself.

Shadowy claws began to beat in frustration at the window and door.

"We need him now," Räv said, drawing her stiletto.

"It's unfortunate because he is the closest, but he's . . . um . . . busy"—Mr. Hu smiled as he glanced around at his friends—"straightening up the chaos we left behind us."

As Räv grew increasingly jumpy, for the next hour the Guardian went on reading his correspondence. Every few minutes some new monster tried to break into the building through glass, wood, or brick but always with the same result.

Only Mr. Hu remained calm, staring with satisfaction at the pile of acceptances. "Everyone I wrote to has replied, and they're willing to listen." He nodded to Räv. "I think you're right: They are as eager for peace as your people are."

"Then this is a historic moment," Monkey said, solemn for once. "The entire world could be changed."

"Even if most of the world will never know." Mistral shrugged.

"Does it matter?" Monkey whistled. "What a triumph for you, Hu, if you can pull it off."

Räv pointed her stiletto outside. "If we don't get help soon, there may not be a meeting. Don't they understand that?"

"Yes, but many of them have to come from China." Mr. Hu's nostrils twitched when a letter materialized that reeked of perfume. "Ah, Master Yen has sent a reply," he said as he plucked it from the air. "If he attends, he has such an inflated image of himself that he'll want to chair the meeting. But I'll make sure to set him straight that that is my right."

When the tiger slit open the letter with a claw, it disappeared in a flash. Then a glow filled the room, slowly materializing into a shining gate of ruby posts with a golden sign above it written in fiery, flashing Chinese characters as well as in English.

CONGRATULATIONS, GREAT GUARDIAN! the sign announced proudly.

Sidney's jaw dropped as he gazed up at it. "Now that's what I call a gate!"

"There are all forms of magic." Mistral sniffed disapprovingly as she shaded her eyes against the light. "Dragons' gates are more for function rather than to impress. Frills are hardly necessary."

Running up to the gate, the rat craned his neck back in awe. "That's where you got it wrong, Mistral old gal. The bigger the person, the bigger the splash. And this one's big enough for a Las Vegas casino."

"And just as garish," Mr. Hu said and whipped his handkerchief from his pocket and covered his muzzle as a thick, cloying perfume, even stronger than the letter's, filled the room. "There are few wizards with magic powerful enough to open a gate all the way from China. But really! This is going overboard, even by *his* standards!"

With his heightened tiger's senses, Tom found himself gagging, and Räv clapped a hand over her nose while Mistral kept trying to clear her nostrils by snorting.

"Keep your voice low," Monkey cautioned. "The gate's open. I hope it's *not* Master Yen." Nervously he touched behind his ear to make sure his hidden staff was there. "He's the last one I wanted to see."

"Well, you did rifle through his workroom during one of your burglaries," Mistral said. She had placed a paw over her own nostrils. "And considering the mischief you've created around the world, there aren't many people who *would* welcome you." Despite her words, she looked worried for her friend.

Through the gate, they heard a man laughing. "You haven't changed, Hu," he said in Chinese. "People expect a little showmanship."

Closing his eyes, the tiger massaged his forehead as if in pain. "At least spare us the fireworks and the doves or whatever other nonsense you have planned."

"They're the best part. You're such a spoilsport, Guardian." The voice sighed in exasperation. "But have it your way."

The thick scent vanished as a white-faced lion with a red mane and blue eyes and black body paced majestically through the gateway and then paused. On his back rode a dumpy little man with a wispy goatee and a blue robe. "If you can pull off an alliance, you'll have performed your greatest act of magic." He began to clap his hands in approval.

"Oh, for Heaven's sake, Yen, will you quit the flattery and move?" an irritated voice boomed as if someone were shouting into an empty steel barrel. "I don't want to stand here all night staring at your robot's rear end!"

"So you brought Ch'ih Yu too." Mr. Hu winced as if he had suddenly developed a headache. "You might have given me a warning so I could have put away the break-ables."

"Well, he just happened to be visiting me to talk about Vatten," Master Yen apologized. "His attacks have gotten bolder. But thanks to you, we have an opportunity to put an end to him." At a tap of his heel, the lion's limbs began to move with a loud creak. The man frowned as he looked down at the right foreleg. "Hmm, that one needs a little oiling."

A callused hand shoved impatiently at the lion's backside, hastening its exit, and then a huge warrior strode through the gate. He was dressed in armor of bronze plates in the shape of maple leaves. Around his wrists were bracelets forged from rings in the shape of more maple leaves. Both the shaft and the leaf-shaped blade of his spear were bronze, as was his head. Only his eyebrows were of iron.

"Well, Hu, do you think we can trust them?" the man

thundered, his voice echoing around the room.

It had gotten rather squeezed with all their guests, and Mr. Hu spread his paws diplomatically. "We will see, Ch'ih Yu. Perhaps it's they who have to learn to trust us."

Master Yen frowned when he saw Monkey, and from somewhere within the lion a device gave out a hollow growl. "You!"

Mr. Hu raised a paw. "He is one of my companions."

Master Yen pressed his lips together in disapproval. "You must have been desperate to have that thief in your home. Don't believe half the things he tells you, and count your valuables when he leaves."

"Is there any place you're welcome?" Tom whispered to the ape.

Monkey shrugged. "I can't help it if I'm misunderstood."

Tom had not seen a statue of either Master Yen or Ch'ih Yu in Chinatown, so he leaned in close to the ape. "Are they some of the 'old ones,' like the Dark Lady?"

Master Yen's ears were sharp and he stared beyond Mr. Hu at the boy. "Who is this, Guardian?"

Mr. Hu placed a paw upon Tom's shoulder. "This is Mistress Lee's grandson Master Thomas. He's now my apprentice." He tapped the back of the boy's head as a reminder. "Mind your manners."

"I would have thought Mistress Lee and you would have taught him better," Master Yen huffed, clearly offended by Tom's ignorance. "Old ones indeed. You'd better not let the Dark Lady hear you."

Ch'ih Yu guffawed and almost knocked Master Yen off the lion when he slapped him on the back. "Well, she is ancient. And so am I. We go back almost to the beginning of the world. And you're nearly as old." He shook his spear. "See this, boy?" He thumped his armored chest. "I was the one who first thought of using metal for weapons. Without me, folks'd still be fighting with rocks and sticks."

"So you've helped people kill each other more efficiently," Master Yen said sarcastically. "That's something to be proud of, to be sure."

The irony was lost on Ch'ih Yu. "Absolutely." He beamed and waved a hand at Master Yen. "And this fellow here knows a few magic tricks." He winked with a squeak. "He's available for parties."

"A few magic tricks?" Master Yen spluttered in outrage, and he leaned so far toward Tom that he almost unseated himself on his own. "I'll have you know that few wizards can match me."

The golden scale on Tom's cheek suddenly caught Ch'ih Yu's eye. "Where'd you get the shiny mole, boy?" he asked, tapping his own cheek with little clinking noises.

Tom felt his face turning red as he tried to answer, and with all the attention turned toward him, he found himself tongue-tied.

"That is the mark of the Empress's favor," Mr. Hu said.

"With her aid, we now share one blood and one soul."

Ch'ih Yu lowered his hand. "Are you sure it's a favor, or is it a curse?"

Master Yen gazed at Tom thoughtfully. "Only time will tell," he said, "but you definitely bear watching, Master Thomas."

Suddenly screeches came from the rooftop. A moment later, howls came from the alley. It was impossible to see anything. But they could hear voices crying, "Freedom!"

"Lady Torka's brought my people to rescue you!" Räv cried excitedly.

Ch'ih Yu hefted his huge spear as if it was a stick. "Well, we can't let them have all the fun, can we, Master Yen?"

"Yes, how would it look at the peace conference if we already owed them a favor?" Master Yen asked amiably as he rolled back his sleeves. "I've a new spell that should do the trick. Come along, Hu, and tell me what you think."

Mr. Hu held up a paw. "Before you go charging out there, how can you tell friend from foe?"

"Shout 'freedom' like they are," suggested Räv.

Master Yen arched an eyebrow, not at all pleased to be receiving orders from a stranger and especially one so young. "And who is this charming young lady?" he asked Mr. Hu.

"This is Mistress Räv, the . . . um . . . ambassador from the rebels," Mr. Hu explained.

"Indeed," Master Yen said, looking down his nose at her.

As if to annoy him further, Räv hooked an arm through Mr. Hu's. "Yes, and the Guardian and I have many matters to discuss. So he won't be going anywhere."

Ch'ih Yu scratched his head, making a sound like someone scouring a copper pot. "It's strange to see a Guardian arm in arm with someone from the Clan of the Nine—"

"We have broken from Vatten," Räv corrected. "We're free people now."

Ch'ih Yu rapped his temple with a hollow bonging sound. "Sorry, it will take a while for that to sink in." He dipped his head as a concession to Räv's title. "But the ambassador is correct, Guardian. It would be best if you stayed in here and kept the phoenix safe."

Master Yen pouted upon his lion. "Oh, very well, I'll tell you what a big success my new spell was as soon as I finish the battle."

There was a good deal of breakage left in Ch'ih Yu's wake as Mr. Hu led them out of the apartment and through the store.

Ch'ih Yu laughed heartily. "Shame on you, Guardian. You shouldn't go around charging a lot of money for something that flimsy. But no harm done? After all, what's the good of being a wizard if you can't fix a few knickknacks, right?"

"The Lore is *not* for household repairs," the Guardian said dourly as he began the task of lifting the wards from the front door, trying his best to ignore the smashing and crashing behind him as Ch'ih Yu examined the store in his own unique way.

The tiger seemed relieved when he could finally open the door. The dark mist spun and twisted as creatures fought within the grayness.

"Freedom!" Master Yen shouted, and kicked his heels against the side of his mount. The lion sprang through the doorway with a loud creak from one leg. Mr. Hu barely had time to whisk an antique teak stool out of the way as Ch'ih Yu bulled after his friend. As it was, he knocked over a screen, a table, and a porcelain drum stool.

As soon as Mr. Hu had closed the door and put the wards back on, he beckoned to Tom. "Master Thomas, please clean up."

Obediently, the boy followed his master into the apartment to fetch the broom . . . when the back of his neck suddenly began to tingle. He glanced around uncomfortably until he finally looked through the apartment doorway and through the store window. Outside he could see flashes in the fog from Master Yen's spells. The feeling, he decided, was a side effect of the wizard's magic.

But then he felt a warmth against his chest. Puzzled, he looked down to see the pouch beginning to rock from side to side on its own. His puzzlement changed to alarm the instant he heard the cracking sound and the tingling on his neck grew into an itching. "Mr. Hu, I . . . I think the egg's broken. It must have happened during the trip."

Mr. Hu held out his paw urgently when he saw something stirring beneath the cloth. "The spells that the dragons cast are finally having an effect. It's hatching. Whatever you do, don't open the pouch."

"Then you take it," Tom said as he took the pouch from around his neck. "You're the Guardian."

Even as he held it in his hands to give it to Mr. Hu, the phoenix began to wriggle violently and the chick forced open the pouch's mouth. Out poked a scrawny head, the red feathers damp and scraggly.

Two little eyes, black and bright as wet beads, stared up at the startled boy. Opening his beak, the phoenix peeped, "Ma . . . Ma . . . Mama."

"No, I'm not," Tom insisted.

"Mama, Mama, Mama," the phoenix cheeped.

Mr. Hu stroked his whiskers thoughtfully. "When some young birds hatch, they imprint on the first creature they see. That means they think that creature is their mother."

"But I can't be a mother," Tom protested. "I'm a boy."

Mr. Hu watched as the scrawny little head rubbed itself against Tom's hand lovingly. "Well, you're one now." Crouching solemnly, he touched his forehead to the floor. "Your Majesty."

Sidney's eyes were wide as he stared at the phoenix. "Jeepers," the rat said, and immediately dropped flat on his belly. Räv simply stood there gaping until Mistral shoved her gently. "Greet the King of all the Birds," the dragon reminded her, and the girl, still stunned, knelt and bent her head.

Mistral's own obeisance was all the more impressive because of her long neck, and she was every inch the duchess. Even Monkey, for once looking very serious, doffed his cap and made his homage.

"Down, Master Thomas," Mr. Hu rumbled. "You are holding royalty."

Tom's knees felt as if they were made of wood; but he forced them to bend so he could get to his knees. The phoenix stared uncomprehendingly over the shelter of his fingers at the kneeling friends. Within Tom's hands, the hatchling was as light as a puff of air and looked so fragile. Outside a creature screeched in rage, and Ch'ih Yu's spear clanged against something.

The noise startled the damp, feathery ball, and instinctively Tom stroked its trembling back and murmured, "It's all right."

But despite his reassuring words, Tom knew that Vatten would use every trick and monster at his disposal to snatch the hatchling from them. Age-old powers would rouse and renew an ancient war. The tiny bird had just swept the world into a new storm of death and terror.

AFTERWORD

L ike a Chinese dragon, the Chinese phoenix differs from his Western counterpart. A Chinese phoenix is reborn but not in flame, and appears only in times of great peace and prosperity. Since he has the power to change malicious people into good ones, he perhaps should be seen as preserving peaceful times.

However, he is a bird, and so I asked myself, What if he imprinted, like some other birds? Could that adopted "parent" use the phoenix for his or her own wicked purposes?

The dragons' uniforms and liveries of coral and barnacles are not traditional to China, but their appearance is inspired by real creatures, aptly named *seadragons*, with their fantastical, colorful appearance. My wife, Joanne Ryder, first called my attention to them, and anyone who wants to see them can go to the National Aquarium in

Baltimore or the Monterey Bay Aquarium, among other places. Dragons are rather vain creatures, so why wouldn't they want to embellish their appearance with ornaments and badges of rank?

My original intention had been to people the dragon kingdom with creatures from the *Shan Hai Ching*, as I had done with the land creatures in the first book in this series, *The Tiger's Apprentice*. However, nothing is quite as strange as the truth, and I have instead based the Winter Palace and its inhabitants as well as the gardens on undersea discoveries. The new generation of submersibles and cameras have let us penetrate into what were once unknown realms of the sea, revealing creatures far more marvelous than anything a writer could imagine. Star rise does indeed occur in the oceans, but in a less spectacular fashion than at the Winter Palace.

Some of the most incredible sea creatures are the siphonophores, and the Nameless One is based on them. Real siphonophores are so fragile that they have not been captured alive; they can grow quite long, but not as gigantic as the monster in this book. Nor do still photographs do justice to these mysterious wonders. They are best seen on videotape, such as the one Bruce Robinson of Monterey Bay Aquarium Research Institute showed during a lecture on the creatures. Anyone who has the privilege of hearing him or seeing his videotapes should do so.